"So, Miss Courtney—yes or no?"

"Let me get this straight. For one week you want me to publicly pretend I'm your mistress." She flicked her eyes up and down his expensive suit, letting them linger on his silk tie. "While you may not be my idea of the ideal date, there must be lots of wome_____ personality in fa_____ I can't believe y_____ the kindness of _____ you've chosen m_____ rescue?"

To her intense fury, he gave a bark of laughter. "Your tongue's got a bite like sulfuric acid."

"All the more reason for you to avoid me."

"Oh, I think I can handle you."

Although born in England, **SANDRA FIELD** has lived most of her life in Canada; she says the silence and emptiness of the north speak to her particularly. While she enjoys traveling, and passing on her sense of a new place, she often chooses to write about the city that is now her home. Sandra says, "I write out of my experience. I have learned that love with its joys and its pains is all-important. I hope this knowledge enriches my writing, and touches a chord in you, the reader."

Books by Sandra Field

HARLEQUIN PRESENTS®
2174—CONTRACT BRIDEGROOM
2144—THE MOTHER OF HIS CHILD

Don't miss any of our special offers. Write to us at the following address for information on our newest releases.

Harlequin Reader Service
U.S.: 3010 Walden Ave., P.O. Box 1325, Buffalo, NY 14269
Canadian: P.O. Box 609, Fort Erie, Ont. L2A 5X3

Sandra Field

THE MISTRESS DEAL

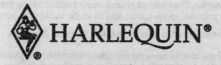

HARLEQUIN®

TORONTO • NEW YORK • LONDON
AMSTERDAM • PARIS • SYDNEY • HAMBURG
STOCKHOLM • ATHENS • TOKYO • MILAN • MADRID
PRAGUE • WARSAW • BUDAPEST • AUCKLAND

If you purchased this book without a cover you should be aware
that this book is stolen property. It was reported as "unsold and
destroyed" to the publisher, and neither the author nor the
publisher has received any payment for this "stripped book."

ISBN 0-373-12215-2

THE MISTRESS DEAL

First North American Publication 2001.

Copyright © 2001 by Sandra Field.

All rights reserved. Except for use in any review, the reproduction or
utilization of this work in whole or in part in any form by any electronic,
mechanical or other means, now known or hereafter invented, including
xerography, photocopying and recording, or in any information storage
or retrieval system, is forbidden without the written permission of the
publisher, Harlequin Enterprises Limited, 225 Duncan Mill Road,
Don Mills, Ontario, Canada M3B 3K9.

All characters in this book have no existence outside the imagination of
the author and have no relation whatsoever to anyone bearing the same
name or names. They are not even distantly inspired by any individual
known or unknown to the author, and all incidents are pure invention.

This edition published by arrangement with Harlequin Books S.A.

® and ™ are trademarks of the publisher. Trademarks indicated with
® are registered in the United States Patent and Trademark Office, the
Canadian Trade Marks Office and in other countries.

Visit us at www.eHarlequin.com

Printed in U.S.A.

CHAPTER ONE

ON THE other side of that door was the enemy.

Lauren Courtney took a deep breath, smoothing the fabric of her skirt with her palm. The enemy. The man who had evidence—entirely fabricated evidence—of a fraud supposedly perpetrated by Lauren's beloved stepfather. Wallace Harvarson a liar? A cheat? Lauren would as soon believe the sun rose in the west.

But Reece Callahan, owner of the huge telecommunications company whose headquarters were in this glittering building in Vancouver, apparently did believe the sun rose in the west. So it was up to Lauren to set him straight. To protect Wallace's reputation now that her stepfather was dead and could no longer speak for himself. That she was gaining entrance to the Callahan stronghold under false pretenses was unfortunate, but necessary; she was under no illusions that a man as ruthless and successful as Reece Callahan would see her otherwise.

Lauren straightened her shoulders, catching a quick glimpse of her reflection in the tall plate-glass windows that overlooked English Bay from the seventh floor. Her chestnut hair was pulled back into a cluster of curls that bared her nape; her suit, a designer label, was severely styled in charcoal-gray, the skirt slit at the back; her blouse was a froth of white ruffles. Italian leather pumps, silver jewelry and dramatic eyeshadow: she'd do. Under normal circumstances she wouldn't be caught dead in charcoal-gray; primary colors were more her forte. But she'd decided back in New York that she needed to look both elegant and composed for this interview. That her heart was pumping rather too fast under her tailored lapel was her secret. A secret she intended to keep.

The receptionist opened the paneled oak door and said politely, "Mr. Callahan, Miss Lauren Courtney is here to see you."

As Lauren stepped inside and the door closed behind her, Reece Callahan got to his feet and walked around his massive mahogany desk, his hand outstretched. "This is indeed a pleasure, Miss Courtney. At your gallery opening in Manhattan last year, when I purchased two of your sculptures, I unfortunately arrived too late to meet you."

While his handclasp was strong, his smile was a mere movement of his lips; his eyes, ice-blue, didn't melt even fractionally. His face was strongly hewn, with a hard jawline, a cleft chin and arrogant cheekbones that instantly Lauren itched to sculpt. His hair, thick with the suggestion of a curl kept firmly under control, was a darker brown than hers. The color of his desk, she thought, polished and sleek.

His body—well, she'd like to sculpt that, too, she realized, her mouth suddenly dry. Beneath his impeccably tailored business suit, she sensed a honed muscularity, a power all the more effective for being hidden.

A cold man. A hard man. Definitely not a man to respond to an appeal to sentiment. Yet sentiment, she thought in sudden despair, was the only weapon she had. He was also several inches taller than her five-foot-nine; she wasn't used to looking so far up, to feeling small, and in consequence at a disadvantage. She didn't like it. Not one bit. Steeling herself, knowing Reece Callahan was indeed the enemy, Lauren detached her fingers from his clasp and said coolly, "I hope you're still enjoying the pieces you purchased?"

"They wear well. I've always liked works in bronze, and yours are particularly fine."

Even though she'd fished for the compliment, it pleased her. "Thank you," she said.

"I'm always glad when my investments do well. The prices you're commanding are escalating very nicely."

Her smile was wiped from her face. "Is that why you bought those bronzes? As an investment?"

"Why else?"

"Not because they spoke to your soul?"

His short laugh held nothing of amusement. "You've got the wrong man."

He'd said a mouthful there. On the basis of the past couple of minutes, Reece Callahan didn't have a soul. But wrong man or not, Lauren was stuck with him. Striving to regain her calm, she said politely, "May I sit down?"

"By all means. Can I get you a coffee?"

"No, thanks." She sat down gracefully in a leather chair, crossing her knees in a swish of silk. "I'm afraid I've obtained this meeting under false pretenses, Mr. Callahan. This isn't a social visit to discuss my work."

"You surprise me—I'd been assuming you were here to solicit a commission. Hawking your wares, so to speak."

Her lashes flickered. "I've never done that yet and see no reason why I should start with you."

"How admirably high-minded of you."

It wasn't part of her strategy to lose her temper before she'd even broached the reason for her visit. Lauren said with a smile as detached as his, "You wouldn't have invested in two of my pieces if you hadn't thought me talented. And even in the worst of times, I've never allowed the whims of the rich to dictate my creativity."

"Then why are you here, Miss Courtney? The rich may

be whimsical, but they also have responsibilities. I, in other words, have a great deal to do today and I'd prefer you to come to the point."

Because he was leaning against the side of his desk, she was forced to look up at him. Her mistake to have sat down, Lauren thought, and said evenly, "I've picked up a rumor—a very distasteful one. I'm trusting you'll reassure me it's nothing but a rumor. In which case I can be out of here in three seconds flat."

She had his full attention; he rapped, "I have much more important things to do with my time than spread rumors. Gossip of any kind has never appealed to me."

"I've heard you're about to publish evidence of fraud on the part of Wallace Harvarson."

He raised one brow. "Ah...now that's no rumor."

Her nails dug into her leather purse. "You cannot possibly have such evidence."

"Why do you say that?"

"He was my stepfather, he would never have been dishonest—I adored him."

"That says more about your lack of perception than about the morals of Wallace Harvarson...clearly you're a better sculptor than a judge of character."

"I knew him through and through!"

"You didn't change your last name to his, though."

"He was my mother's second husband," Lauren said tightly. "My own father died when I was three. Although she divorced Wallace when I was twelve, he and I stayed in touch over the years. As you no doubt know, he died fourteen months ago. Obviously he can't defend himself against this ridiculous charge. So I'm here to do so in his place."

"And what form does this defense take?"

She leaned forward, speaking with passionate intensity.

"My own knowledge of the kind of man he was. Altogether I knew him for nineteen years, and I can tell you it's impossible he would have lied and cheated and stolen money."

"My dear Miss Courtney, that's a very touching response. Although a few tears might improve it. Tears or no, such a reply is meaningless in a court of law. I plan to publish the legal evidence for Wallace Harvarson's fraud next week, and in so doing clear the name of one of my companies. I will not tolerate being seen in the business world as less than honest. Which was your stepfather's legacy to me."

Appalled, she whispered, "*Publish* it? You can't mean that!"

"I mean every word." Reece Callahan drew back his sleeve, looking at his gold watch. "If that's all you have to say, I think we can profitably terminate this interview."

With swift grace, Lauren got to her feet. "If you publish such outright lies about my stepfather, I'll sue you for defamation of character."

"Please don't—you'd be laughed out of court. Besides, do you have any idea what that would cost you?"

"Does everything come down to money with you?"

"In this case, yes—Wallace Harvarson milked my company of five hundred thousand dollars."

"What's the truth, Mr. Callahan? That you made a bad business decision that cost you half a million and now you're looking for a scapegoat?"

"You go public with a statement like that and I'll be the one suing you," he said in a voice like steel. "My secretary will see you out."

"I'm not leaving until you promise you won't drag my stepfather's name through the mud for your own ends!"

He straightened, taking a step toward her. "You really

do have gall, Miss Courtney. I happen to know you bought your studio with your inheritance from your stepfather, and that you're still the owner of a very nice little property on the coast of Maine that belonged to him."

Her brain made a lightning-fast leap. "You've known all along that I'm Wallace's stepdaughter?"

"I always research the artists I'm investing in—it makes good business sense."

"So you've been leading me on ever since I got here—how despicable!"

"That label belongs to you rather than me. You're the one who's been living off the proceeds of fraud. I suppose it beats doing the starving-sculptor-in-a-garret routine. Even if your artistic integrity is a touch tarnished."

White with rage, Lauren spat, "My integrity isn't the issue here—what about yours? Smearing the reputation of a dead man in the full knowledge that I can't possibly hire the kind of lawyers you can afford...doesn't that give your conscience even the smallest twinge?"

His blue eyes were fastened on her face; he said in a peculiar voice, "You really do believe he's innocent, don't you?"

"Of course I do! Do you think I'd be wasting my time, let alone yours, if I thought for one moment Wallace could have done anything so underhanded?"

"Then I'm sorry. Because you're in for a rude awakening. And now I really must ask you to leave—I have an appointment in ten minutes."

Hating herself for doing so, knowing she had no other choice, Lauren swallowed her pride. "Is there nothing I can do to make you change your mind?"

"Not a thing."

"There must be something..."

His eyes like gimlets, he said, "I'm surprised, with your reputation, that you haven't offered the obvious."

Lauren flushed. "My sexual reputation, you mean?"

"Precisely."

Her fists were clenched at her sides so hard the knuckles were white. "So you researched that, too. And along with the rest of the world, you believed every word the gutter press printed about me. Fabrications my mentor Sandor fed his journalist friends. Yet you're the one who says he doesn't believe in gossip?"

"Your mentor's highly respected."

"Whereas I was a mere upstart with the kind of looks the press adores. Do you wonder why I'm begging you not to publish all these lies about Wallace? I know the power of the media to ruin reputations...know it and fear it and have suffered from it."

"When I arrived at your gallery last year, you were leaving by another door. Arm in arm with two men, no less. I doubt that your lack of morals is just gossip invented by a vengeful ex-lover."

Her shoulders sagged. "I didn't come here to defend myself against promiscuity," she said in a low voice. "Neither did I come to say I'd sleep with you if you promised not to publish."

"So why didn't you sue Sandor—your ex-lover, your ex-teacher, your mentor—if he was lying?"

"It was four years ago," she blazed. "At that time I'd sold exactly two pieces in my whole life—I wasn't into selling then, I knew I hadn't reached the point where I wanted my stuff out there in the real world—as it happens, I do have artistic integrity, Mr. Callahan. Short of asking Wallace for money, I didn't have one cent to rub against another. And lawyers come expensive. As you know."

"Indeed." Hands in his pockets, Reece looked her up

and down with a deliberation that made her flinch inwardly; she felt as though his ice-cold eyes were stripping her naked. But Lauren had toughened in the years since Sandor had set out to drag her through the gutter personally and artistically; she raised her chin, breathing hard, and said not one word. He said noncommittally, "You're not dressed cheaply."

"There are some wonderful secondhand places in Greenwich Village. I know them all."

"I see." Casually Reece leaned back against the desk again. "Perhaps I should reconsider."

In a flash of incredulous hope, she said eagerly, "You mean you believe me about Wallace?"

"That's not what I mean at all. But there is something you could do for me. A way in which you could be useful to me."

The light died from her face. "And in return, you wouldn't publish anything about my stepfather?"

"That's correct."

She said in a level voice, "I won't sleep with you, Mr. Callahan."

"I'm not asking you to, Miss Courtney."

"Soiled goods," she said bitterly.

"As you say."

Briefly she closed her eyes. "Then what do you want of me?"

"You could be of use to me for the next week or so—after that I'm off to London and Cairo. But while I'm here, I have a number of engagements that mix business with pleasure, never my favorite way of operating but sometimes it's unavoidable. I'd want you to pose as my companion. My lover, to put it bluntly. I can't imagine you'd find that difficult."

Her response came from a deep place she couldn't have named or ignored. "No! I'm a sculptor—not a call girl."

"Either you want to protect your stepfather, or you don't. Which is it?"

His voice was clipped, utterly emotionless. She flashed, "Why would you want to be seen with someone whose reputation's not much better than a call girl's?"

"Because you interest me."

"Oh, that's just lovely. As if I'm a stock market quote. Or a microchip."

"You're a very talented woman. As well you know. You're also articulate, well-dressed and pretty enough for my purposes. In other words, you'll do. So which is it, Miss Courtney—yes or no?"

Pretty enough, she thought in true fury. She wasn't just pretty, she was beautiful: without a speck of vanity she knew this, for her mirror and the rest of the world had told her so often enough. But to Mr. Ice-Water-In-His-Veins Callahan she was merely pretty.

Not that that was the real issue, Lauren realized hastily.

She dragged her thoughts back to Wallace, his quicksilver smile and ready laughter, the way that his rare and always delightful visits had rescued her from an adolescence that had been rife with real unhappiness. Her mother had resented her burgeoning beauty, while her mother's third husband had despised her budding talent; between them, they had made her teenage years a misery. She'd left home the week she'd graduated from high school; it had been Wallace who'd seen to it that she hadn't starved in a garret during the years when she'd been studying at art school, sculpting all hours of the night, and gradually unearthing her own strengths.

And weaknesses. Of which Sandor was the prime example.

This was no time to think about Sandor. She said carefully, "Let me get this straight. For one week you want me to publicly pretend I'm your mistress." She flicked her eyes up and down his expensive suit, letting them linger on his silk tie, which bore the crest of a very distinguished university. "While you may not be *my* idea of the ideal date, there must be lots of women who'd bypass your personality in favor of your money. Since I can't believe you're offering this out of the kindness of your heart, I wonder why you've chosen me to come to your rescue?"

To her intense fury, he gave a bark of laughter. "Your tongue's got a bite like sulfuric acid."

"All the more reason for you to avoid me."

"Oh, I think I can handle you."

Discovering a profound wish to knock him off balance, she said sweetly, "You're forgetting something. You're a big name, with your mergers and your innovations and your huge profits—don't think I hadn't done *my* research. As for me, I had a major show in London last year, and I have a growing reputation in the States. If you and I pose as lovers, the press will have a field day. There will be gossip, Mr. Callahan. Lots of lovely gossip."

"So your answer's no." He moved toward the door. "Don't forget to buy Wednesday's paper, will you? You'll see a whole new side to your stepfather, and—trust me—it won't be based on gossip."

She couldn't bear that. She couldn't. Her only alternative was to toe the line. Do as Reece Callahan had proposed. Because Lauren was under no illusions; even if she could afford to sue Reece, and even if by some remote chance she won, the damage would have been done. Wallace's name would always be linked with dishonor. She said coldly, "I was merely pointing out the pitfalls of your course of action."

"How altruistic of you."

"If I do this, it would be an act. Only an act. In private I wouldn't allow you to come within ten feet of me."

"You're assuming I'd want to."

Her breath hissed between her teeth. "Tell me precisely what you'd require of me."

"You'd stay in my condo near Stanley Park. On Saturday you'd go with me to a cocktail party and dinner that I'm hosting. One of my CEOs is laboring under the delusion that his daughter would make me a fine wife. Your presence will disabuse him of that notion. Then on Sunday there's a private dinner party at the home of a man I'm thinking of bringing on board. Unfortunately his wife is more interested in me than in her husband's career. You'll give her the message I'm not available. Two days later we'll fly to my house in Whistler—I don't often go there this time of year, I use it mainly for skiing in February. But I'll be doing business with some Japanese software experts—and you'd host their wives. Then we go to a yacht club off the east coast of Vancouver Island, where I'm to meet an associate in the commodity market. After that, it's back here and you can go your own way." He paused. "Eight days, not counting tomorrow."

Lauren's adventurous spirit, never much in abeyance, quickened. She'd heard of Whistler, the luxurious ski resort north of the city; and she'd never been to Vancouver Island, set like a green jewel in the waters of the Pacific Ocean. Keeping her face impassive, she said, "I get the message. Because you're rich, a lot of women are after you."

He raised one brow. "You could call it an occupational hazard."

She almost smiled, feeling the first twinge of liking for him. Shoving it down, she said crisply, "If I choose to do this, I need to make something clear—I'm not after you, no matter how much money you have. In public, I'll do my best to convince the world that you and I are madly in love. In private, I'll require a room of my own and strict boundaries around my privacy.''

"I assure you," Reece said silkily, "that will be no problem.''

He found her undesirable. A turnoff. That's what he meant. Stifling a surge of rage as fierce as it was irrational, Lauren said, "I'd also require a signed statement from you that you would never, directly or indirectly, damage my stepfather's name.''

"Providing you keep to the terms of our agreement.''

Her turquoise eyes flung themselves like waves of the sea against the hard planes of his face. "I would. I promise.''

"So you're saying you'll do it?''

She bit her lip. "We'd never bring it off—it's so obvious we don't like each other.''

"You're being too diplomatic. Mutual antipathy—wouldn't that be a more accurate description?''

"It would, yes," she snapped. "Plus, to put it bluntly, you don't look like you could act your way out of a paper bag.''

"You let me worry about that," he retorted. "Yes or no? Eight days of your time or your stepfather's reputation—which is it to be?''

"I'll do it," she said. "You've known all along that I would.''

"So you're astute as well as talented.''

"You're getting a bargain," she mocked.

"We'll see," he said dryly. "In addition to our basic agreement, I'll require you to sign a statement that you'll never discuss our supposed relationship with the press.

Come to this office at three tomorrow afternoon. I'll have the documents drawn up for us both to sign. You can arrive at my condo at ten tomorrow night—I'm out earlier in the evening."

"Very well." Lauren gave him a derisive smile. "I do hope all this acting won't be too taxing for you."

"If you're asking for a demonstration, you're out of luck. I don't believe in wasted action."

She clenched her fists. "Your secretary must know we're not lovers—that we just met this morning."

"My secretary is very well paid to keep her mouth shut."

"Now why should I be surprised?" Lauren said cordially. "Goodbye, Mr. Callahan. I won't say it's been a pleasure."

"Don't push your luck—the document's not signed yet."

She said tartly, "If Wallace is looking down on me from heaven, I hope he appreciates what I'm doing for him."

"People who cheat and lie don't go to heaven." Reece opened the door. "Goodbye."

They were in full view of his secretary. "Then I guess you won't go there, either," Lauren said, reaching up and kissing him on both cheeks. "Goodbye, darling," she added in a carrying voice. "I'll see you tomorrow."

Pivoting, she smiled at the secretary. "I'll see myself out," she said, and walked toward the elevator. The slit in her skirt, she knew, showed her legs rather admirably. To her great satisfaction she heard Reece Callahan's door snap shut with more force than was required.

At least she'd achieved that much.

Had she ever in her life conceived such an overwhelming dislike for a man? Even Edward, her mother's third husband, liked dogs and rhododendrons, and laughed loudly at his own jokes. Reece Callahan wouldn't know how to laugh.

Cold. Hard. Manipulative.

She was going to read both documents very carefully before she signed anything.

CHAPTER TWO

CHARLOTTE BOND, better known as Charlie, said incredulously, "You agreed to do *what?*"

"You heard," Lauren said. "I agreed to act as Reece Callahan's mistress, in public only, for the space of one week. Well, eight days. That's all. It's no big deal."

"Lauren, I dated Reece. Twice. He plays major league. And he's got a hole where his heart's supposed to be."

"So why did you date him twice?"

A rueful grin lit up Charlie's piquant face. "I couldn't believe that a guy with those rugged, damn-your-eyes kind of good looks could really be as cold as the proverbial glacier."

"You saw him as a challenge."

"I guess so." Charlie gave a snort of self-derision. "What a joke. Although we did have a few things in common."

Charlie was a top-notch tax consultant, whose logical brain was the antithesis of Lauren's: they had a friendship of opposites that had survived Charlie's move from New York to Canada's west coast last summer. "Don't you see?" Lauren said equably. "It's because he's such a cold fish that I feel quite safe taking this on. No risk Reece Callahan's going to lose his head over me. We'll act as lovers in public, go our separate ways in private, and Wallace's good name will be safe. Simple."

Charlie grimaced. "Trouble is, I feel responsible. If I hadn't brought up Wallace's name quite innocently to Reece, in connection with that software company Wallace was involved with, Reece wouldn't have mentioned I should keep my ear to the ground for some very interesting revelations about Wallace. None of which were to Wallace's credit. As soon as he said that, all my alarm bells went off and that's when I phoned you.''

"You and I were due for a visit anyway," Lauren said comfortingly. "And I'm so glad I've finally made it to the west coast. Oh, Charlie, it's wonderful to have a bit of money to spend! To be able to get on a plane and fly here and not have to worry about the cost. For so many years I've been rock-bottom broke, having to count every cent I spent."

But Charlie was still frowning. "Just so long as you don't get hurt."

"By Reece Callahan?" Lauren made a very rude noise. "Not a chance. Did I tell you he bought those two bronze pieces as an investment? They're two of my best works, and yet they're owned by a man who doesn't give a damn about what they say—his only concern is that they increase in value. And you're worried I might fall for him? Huh. Pigs might fly."

Charlie sighed. "It's an awful waste. He's got a great body."

"To sculpt, yes. To go to bed with? No, ma'am. Anyway, I'm off sex, have been for years."

Charlie took a big gulp of her Chardonnay, her face still troubled. "You're absolutely certain of Wallace's innocence?"

"Of course I am!"

"You did tell me once that your inheritance from him was less than you'd expected."

"That's true enough. And his mother's jewels that he'd promised me, they never did turn up. But, Charlie, everyone can have setbacks on the financial markets, you know that from your own work. It doesn't mean the person's committed fraud.''

"He never confided in you?"

Lauren's brow crinkled in thought. "We didn't talk about stuff like that. Serious stuff." Her voice wobbled. "He was such fun, always laughing or singing pop songs at the top of his lungs—I miss him so much.''

"Mmm…" Charlie ran her fingers through her tousled blond curls. "Just make sure you look after yourself as far as Reece is concerned. And read all the fine print on these documents you're going to sign."

"I will." Lauren grinned at her friend.

"Let's go out for supper, I don't feel like cooking. There's a divine Czech restaurant just down the road."

"And neither of us will mention Reece Callahan's name again. Okay?"

"Okay," said Charlie. Nor did they.

Promptly at three o'clock the next afternoon, Lauren presented herself to Reece's secretary. The October day had turned unexpectedly warm; her dress was a chic linen sheath in deep blue with long sleeves. Gold hoops that Wallace had given her for her eighteenth birthday swung at her lobes, and she'd pulled her hair back with a gold clip. Her makeup was dramatic, that and her dress making her eyes look almost indigo.

The secretary said pleasantly, "Mr. Callahan shouldn't be too long, Miss Courtney—but he is running a little behind schedule."

So she was to be kept waiting like a common supplicant? Like a patient at the dentist's? Which was just how she felt: all her nerves on edge, dread like a lump in the pit of her stomach. Lauren said, "Oh, I'm sure he doesn't mean to keep me waiting, Miss Riley. I'll go straight in."

"I don't think—"

But Lauren was already opening Reece's door. He was seated in front of his computer screen and looked up in annoyance. She said with warm intimacy, "Hello, darling—I knew you wouldn't want me to sit outside…how are you?" Then, as she closed the door, she gave him a wicked grin, her voice going back to normal. "I should tell you that at the age of thirteen I planned to become the second Sarah Bernhardt. I could get to enjoy this."

He said curtly, "The first thing you'd better learn is never to interrupt me when I'm working."

"But, dearest," she cooed, batting her artfully mascaraed lashes, "I'm your heart's delight."

For a split second Lauren thought she caught a flash of emotion deep in Reece's eyes. But then it was gone. If indeed it had existed. He said sharply, "I mean it, Lauren."

"What a dull life you must lead."

He surged to his feet. He'd discarded his jacket and tie; his shirt, open at the throat, revealed a tangle of dark hair. "Let's get something straight," he said with dangerous softness. "I'm the one with the evidence about Wallace. So I get to call the shots."

Her chin lifted mutinously. "I don't like being told what to do."

"Then you'd better learn fast."

"I think you're forgetting something, Reece—this is a reciprocal deal. You've got something I want and I've got something you want. So both of us get to call the shots."

"There can't be two bosses—that's a basic corporate rule."

"We're not talking corporations, we're talking love at first sight. Passion, adoration and lust." She gave him a complacent smile. "The rules are different."

"Certainly that's your area of expertise."

She flushed. "Let's get something else straight. Right now. You can quit throwing my reputation in my face."

"What's that cliché? If the shoe fits..."

So angry she forgot all caution, Lauren blazed, "If you think for one minute that I'm going to let you walk all over me for eight consecutive days, you'd better think again. Because I'm not. No chance."

"You look rather more than pretty when you're angry," he remarked. "How do you look when you're making love?"

"*You'll* never find out!"

"According to the media, you wouldn't know how. To make love, I mean. You use a guy, milk him dry, then go on to the next one. Which can hardly be dignified by the word *love*." He closed the distance between them, taking her by the shoulders with cruel strength, his eyes boring into hers. "What I don't understand is how you can create works of art that breathe truth and morality from such a shoddy little soul. Or why, when you're so extraordinarily talented, you play cheap sexual games to further your career."

She flinched; in attacking her work, he was stabbing her where she was most vulnerable. She said fiercely, "I came here to sign a couple of documents, not to have my character torn to shreds by a man who wouldn't recognize an emotion if it hit him in the face. Especially if that emotion was called love."

As suddenly as he had seized her, Reece let her go. "You don't have an answer for me, do you?"

"My character and my sculptures are entirely congruent."

"Oh, for God's sake."

She said with sudden insight, "You know what your

problem is? You're not used to people contradicting you. Especially a woman. I bet you're surrounded day and night by *yes, sir, no, sir, whatever you say, sir.* Very bad for you.''

''Whereas you're surrounded by men who fall all over you, agreeing with every word you say just so long as they end up in your bed.''

Anger flicked along her nerves. She said amicably, ''Reece, I'll spell it out for you again. Please don't spend the whole week harping on my love affairs—I have a low tolerance for boredom.''

''Is that a challenge, Miss Courtney?''

''It's a statement of fact.''

''Frankly, I don't care if you're bored out of your skull the entire eight days. Just as long as you do what I say.'' Reece pulled open a drawer and extracted two sheets of typescript. ''Read this. There are two copies, one for each of us. I'll get my secretary to witness our signatures.''

The document, in carefully worded legalese, said that Lauren Courtney would present herself in the public realm as Reece Callahan's lover for a period of eight days, and would preserve total confidentiality about the contents of this agreement in perpetuity. In return, Reece Callahan contracted never to publish anything of any nature about Wallace Harvarson, stepfather of the aforesaid Lauren Courtney.

The language, while cumbersome, was clear. Lauren said steadily, ''I'm ready to sign if you are.''

Reece folded the papers to hide the text and pressed a buzzer on his desk. A few moments later the secretary walked in. ''I'd like you to witness our signatures, Shirley, please,'' Reece said. ''Lauren?''

Once she signed, she was committed. For a few seconds that felt like hours, Lauren stared at him blankly. Was she mad promising to live for over a week with a man who was the antithesis of everything she believed in? What did she really know about him? Maybe the moment she walked in the door of his condo, he'd fall on her. And what recourse would she have? If she didn't stay for the full eight days, he'd publish a bunch of scurrilous lies about Wallace. Charlie had tried to warn her that Reece would be a formidable foe. But had Lauren listened? Oh, no.

"Lauren?" Reece said more sharply. "You have to sign in both places."

Yes, sir, she thought crazily, picked up his platinum pen and signed each copy. Then she watched as Reece added a totally illegible scrawl, and the secretary her ultraneat script. The secretary then left the room, never once having looked Lauren in the eye.

It was done. She was committed.

Reece said irritably, "This is a business deal that will terminate a week from tomorrow. Stop looking at me as though you've just married me for life."

She blurted, "Have you ever been married?"

"Are you kidding?"

"Yes or no will do."

"No."

"Neither have I... Sandor had a soul above such petty, bourgeois standards."

"Lauren," Reece said coldly, "signing those forms wasn't a license for true confessions."

"Wasn't a license for you to behave like a human being, you mean?"

"We're not in public. We don't have to act."

"If I stuck a pin in you, would you bleed?" she demanded in true exasperation. "Or would ice water drip on the carpet?"

"It irks the hell out of you that I'm not bowled over by you, doesn't it?"

Truth. That's what she sought in her work, and that's how she endeavored to live her life. Lauren said concisely, "You insist on seeing me as something I'm not, and you've built such a barrier between yourself and the real world that you treat everything and everyone in terms of either monetary value or functionality. That's what irks the hell out of me."

His mouth hardened. He said brusquely, "Here's my card with my condo address and phone number. I've opened a couple of accounts for you downtown in case you need clothes—the details are on this piece of paper. And this is your copy of our agreement. Ten o'clock tonight, Lauren. Please don't be late."

Automatically she took the papers he was holding out and shoved them in her purse. "I'll be there."

He stepped back, holding her gaze with his own. "One more thing. You're the most beautiful woman I've ever seen."

As her jaw dropped, he opened the door. "See you tonight, darling," he added, giving her a smile of such breathtaking intimacy that her heart lurched in her breast. Speechless, she dragged her eyes away and walked past the secretary like a woman in a dream. The elevator was waiting for her. As the doors slid open, she heard the soft closing of Reece's door behind her.

You're pretty enough.

You're the most beautiful woman I've ever seen.

Which was the truth and which was an act? And if she couldn't tell the difference, what had she let herself in for?

The cab swung into the grounds of Reece's condo at fifteen minutes to ten that evening. Lauren, though she had difficulty admitting this to herself, hadn't wanted to be late. In consequence she'd allowed extra time for traffic. Too much time, she realized, paying the taxi driver, and taking her big suitcase from him. She noticed that the grounds had been designed with a Japanese theme, a harmony of rock, fern and shrub overlaid by the gentle ripple of water. An island of peace, Lauren thought, and wished she felt more peaceful.

She felt anything but peaceful.

If she arrived early, would Reece think she was too eager for his company? She could simply stand here for the next ten minutes and admire the garden.

To heck with that. No games, no pretense. She headed for the lobby, where the uniformed desk attendant recognized her name immediately, and called the elevator for her. "Mr. Callahan is expecting you, madam," he said with a pleasant smile. "The top floor."

She gave him an equally pleasant smile back, wondering why she should feel like a high-class call girl when she was anything but. The elevator smoothly deposited her outside double doors with exquisite wrought-iron handles; Reece's unit was the only one on this floor. Her feet sinking in the thick carpeting, Lauren pushed the bell. Let the adventure begin, she thought, and fixed her smile on her face.

CHAPTER THREE

REECE swung the door open. For the space of five full seconds Lauren stared at him, all her rehearsed greetings fleeing her mind. He was naked to the waist and barefoot, his hair wet and tousled. Detail after detail emblazoned itself on her brain: the pelt of dark hair on his deep chest; his taut, corded belly; the elegant flow of muscle and bone from throat to shoulder. He said flatly, "You're early."

"I allowed too much time for the traffic."

"You'd better come in—I just got out of the shower."

His jeans were low-slung, his jaw shadowed with a day's beard. He looked like a human being, Lauren thought, her mouth dry. He also looked extraordinarily and dangerously sexy. "Here," he said, "let me take your suitcase."

She surrendered it without a murmur, staring at the ripple of muscles above his navel as if she'd never seen a half-naked man before. As Reece turned his back to her, putting the case down, the long curve of his spine made her feel weak at the knees. Only because she was an artist, she thought frantically. Nothing to do with being a woman in the presence of an overpowering masculinity. Yet why hadn't she realized in his office how beautifully he moved, with an utterly male economy and grace?

He said, "I might as well show you your room right away. What's in the other bag?"

In her left hand Lauren was clutching a worn leather briefcase. "My tools...I never travel without them."

"Here, give them to me."

"I'll carry them." She managed a faint smile. "I've had some of them for years."

"You don't trust me, do you?" he rasped. "Not even with something as simple as a bag of tools."

"Reece," she said vigorously, "the agreement is to act like lovers in public. Not to fight cat-and-dog in private."

He looked her up and down, from her ankle-height leather boots and dark brown tights to her matching ribbed turtleneck and faux fur jacket with its leopard pattern of big black spots. "You're obviously the cat. So does that make me the dog?"

"You're no poodle."

"A basset hound?"

She chuckled, entering into the spirit of the game. "You have very nice ears and your legs are too long. Definitely not a basset."

"Do you realize we're actually agreeing about something?"

"And I'm scarcely in the door," she said demurely, wondering with part of her brain how she could have said that about his ears.

"Let me take your coat."

As she put down her tools and slid her jacket from her shoulders, her breasts lifting under her sweater, he said, "I wondered if you'd back out at the last minute."

The smile faded from her face. "So that you could blacken Wallace's name from one end of the country to the other? I don't think so. Which room is mine?"

"At the end of the hall."

For the first time, Lauren took stock of her surroundings. Her initial impression was of space; and of some wonderful oak and leather furniture by a modern Finnish designer whom she'd met once at a showing in Manhattan. Then her gaze took in the collection of art that filled the space with color, movement and excitement. She said dazedly, "That's a Kandinsky. A Picasso. A Chagall. And surely that collage is James Ardmore. Reece, it's a wonderful piece, I know he's not very popular, but I'm convinced he's the real thing. And look, a Pirot, don't you love the way his sculptures catch the light no matter where you stand?"

Her face lit with enthusiasm, she walked over to the gleaming copper coils, caressing them gently with her fingertips. When she looked up, Reece was watching her, his expression inscrutable. She said eagerly, "It begs to be touched, don't you think? I adore his stuff."

"I have another of his works. In my bedroom."

She didn't even stop to think. "Can I see it?"

Reece led the way down a wide hallway, where more paintings danced in front of her dazzled gaze. His bedroom windows overlooked the spangled avenues in Stanley Park; but Lauren had eyes only for the bronze sculpture of a man that stood on a pedestal by the balcony doors. She let her hands rest on the man's bare shoulders, her eyes half shut as she traced the taut tendons. "It's as though Pirot creates something that's already there," she whispered, "just waiting for him."

Reece said harshly, "Is that how you make love?"

Her head jerked 'round. Jamming her hands in her pockets, she said, "What do you mean?"

"Sensual. Rapt. Absorbed."

She'd hated being anywhere near Sandor's bed by the end of the relationship. Not that Reece needed to know that. "How I do or do not make love is none of your concern."

"So what are you doing in my bedroom?"

The bedside lamp cast planes of light and shadow across Reece's bare chest; Lauren was suddenly aware that she was completely alone with him only feet from the wide bed in which he slept. "You think it was a come-on, me asking to see the sculpture?" she cried. "Do you have to cheapen everything?"

As if the words were wrenched from him, he said, "I bought the condo new just ten months ago. You're the only woman to have ever been in this room."

She knew instantly that he was telling the truth; although she couldn't have said where that knowledge came from. Frightened out of all proportion, she took two steps backward. "It doesn't matter if you've had fifty women in your bedroom," she said in a thin voice. "I haven't slept with anyone since Sandor and I'm certainly not going to start with you."

"You expect me to believe that?"

"I don't care if you do or not!"

"But that was four years ago and—"

"Three years and ten months," she interrupted furiously, "and what business is it of yours anyway?"

"None. I'll show you to your room."

If eyes were the windows of the soul, Lauren thought fancifully, then Reece had just closed the shutters. But did he have a soul? He certainly had emotions. She'd learned that much in the last few minutes.

She trailed after him, noticing another Picasso sketch on his bedroom wall, as well as a delightful Degas impression of a dancer. Reece was striding down the hallway as though pursued by a hungry polar bear. About to hurry after him, Lauren suddenly came to a halt. In a lit alcove in the wall stood a small Madonna and child, carved in wood so old its patina was almost black. The figures were simply, rather crudely carved; yet such a radiant tenderness flowed from one to the other that Lauren felt emotion clog her throat.

She wasn't even aware of Reece walking back to where she was standing. He said roughly, "What's the matter?"

"It's so beautiful," she whispered, her eyes filled with wonderment.

"Unknown artist, late fourteenth century. You can pick it up, if you want to."

"But—"

"Lauren, pick it up."

With a kind of reverence she lifted the statue, her hands curling around it with the same tenderness that infused the figures. "Look how her shoulder curves into her arm and then into the child's body," she said. "Whoever carved it must have loved his child...don't you think?" She lifted her face to Reece, a face open and unguarded, totally without guile.

Briefly he rested his hand on her cheek. He said thickly, "You could have been the model. For the mother."

"That's a lovely thing to say..."

The warmth from his touch coursed through her veins; he was standing very close to her. And this was the man she'd thought bore no resemblance to a human being? A man who had no soul? "Wherever did you find it?" she asked, wanting to prolong a moment that felt both fragile and of enormous significance.

"In a little village in Austria—way off the beaten track."

"Would you mind if I made a copy of it? I'd destroy the copy once it was finished." Very gently she put the carving back in its niche.

"I'll be out every day," Reece said. "You can do what you like."

She glanced up. The shutters were back, she thought in true dismay; his face had closed against her. Her question came from nowhere, the words out before she could stop them. "Did your mother love you, Reece?"

He said with deadly quietness, "You have no right to ask that question and I have no intention of answering it."

"I guess I—"

"Your room's at the end of the hall. Do you want anything to eat or drink before you go to bed?"

"I'm not a child to be sent to bed because she's misbehaved!"

"No. You're an intrusive and insensitive young woman."

"If you have problems with my question, then say so. But don't blame me for asking it."

"We have a business arrangement—nothing more. Kindly remember that, will you?"

Lauren said evenly, "Years ago, I allowed Sandor to cower me into submission over and over again...and I almost lost myself in the process. I vowed I'd never let that happen again. So don't try, Reece—it won't wash."

"We're fighting cat-and-dog again. And that's not in the agreement, isn't that what you said?"

He was right; she had. "There's something about you," she said tightly. "You're like a chunk of ironwood. Or a length of steel."

"Just don't think you can shape me to your ends."

"Do you despise all women? Or is it just me?"

"You never let up, do you?" he said unpleasantly.

She paled, suddenly remembering the statue in his bedroom. "Oh. You prefer men."

"I do not prefer men! It's very simple, Lauren. I've got no use for all the posturing and stupidities that masquerade in our society as romance."

"That carving of the Madonna and child—it's not about romance. It's about love."

"Love—what do you know about love? Do you have a husband? Do you have a child?"

She winced, her face suddenly pinched and pale. "You know I don't," she said in a stony voice. "I loved Sandor. But he didn't want marriage or children. Or me. The real me."

"You sure know when to pull out all the stops," Reece said nastily. "You can make tea or coffee in your room. I eat breakfast at six-thirty and I'm gone by seven. I'll be back tomorrow evening at six, cocktails at seven, dinner afterward. Wear something dressy. Did you buy yourself some clothes?"

"Of course not," she said shortly.

"You've got to look the part, Lauren! As well as act it."

She took refuge in a matching anger. "I have my own money, and if I need clothes I'll buy them myself."

"Do you have to argue about everything?" he snarled.

"With you, yes."

"I should have asked for character references before I signed that goddamned agreement."

"Adversity might teach you a thing or two," she retorted. "I'm going to bed. Good night."

"Be ready by quarter to seven tomorrow evening."

"Yes, Reece, I'll be ready." And wearing the most outrageous outfit I own, she thought vengefully. She turned away, marching toward the door at the end of the hall, and heard him say behind her, "I'll bring your case down. And your tools—if you trust me to, that is."

So much for the grand exit, Lauren thought with a quiver of inner laughter; she'd forgotten about her suitcase. "That far I trust you," she said.

Her bedroom was painted terra-cotta, the bedspread and drapes in shades of teal blue, the whole effect confident

yet full of welcome. Two exquisite Chinese scrolls hung
on either side of the marble fireplace, while the shelves
held an enviable collection of Ming pottery. Aware
through every nerve of Reece's footsteps as he entered her
room, she turned to face him. He said evenly, ''That door
leads to the bathroom, and the balcony's over there. I'll
see you tomorrow evening around six or six-thirty.''

He didn't want to see her in the morning, that was obvious. She leaned over to switch on a lamp, her hair swinging softly around her face. ''Enjoy your day,'' she said
with the merest breath of sarcasm.

For a full five seconds Reece stared at her in silence.
She raised her chin, refusing to look away, wishing with
all her heart that he'd put a shirt on. Then he said crisply,
''Good night, Lauren,'' and closed the door with a decisive
snap.

Lauren sank down on the wide bed, knowing she'd give
almost anything to be back in the unpretentious guest bedroom in Charlie's apartment. Anything but Wallace's reputation, she thought unhappily.

Eight days wasn't long. She could manage. Even if
Reece Callahan repulsed and attracted her in equal measure.

It would be a great deal safer if she were indifferent to
him.

Lauren woke early the next morning. The sun was streaming through the French doors that led onto the balcony and
she knew exactly what she was going to do all day. But
she'd need a key to Reece's condo.

Quickly she dressed in her leggings and sweater. In her
bare feet, her hair loose around her face, she hurried down
the hall, not even glancing at the statue of the Madonna:

she'd have lots of time for that. In the spacious living room, she called, "Reece? Are you up?"

"In the kitchen."

He didn't sound exactly welcoming. Pasting a smile on her face, she walked into an ultramodern kitchen equipped with what seemed like acres of stainless steel. Reece was, thank goodness, wearing a shirt. He was munching on a piece of toast, gazing at the papers strewn over one of the counters. She said, "You start early."

"So, apparently, do you. What do you want?"

"A key—I need to go out this morning."

"The doorman has an extra, I've told him to give it to you." He shifted one of the papers, making a note with the pen in his free hand.

"That toast smells good," she said provocatively. "I think I'll have some."

"Can't you wait until I've gone?"

"Are you always cranky in the morning?"

"Not with people I like."

"Try harder," Lauren said, glaring at him as she headed for the coffee machine.

His voice like a whiplash, he said, "Sandor's beginning to have all my sympathy."

The mug she was filling almost slipped from her grasp; scalding liquid splashed the back of her hand. With a gasp of pain, she banged the mug down on the counter and ran for the sink, where she turned on the cold tap and thrust her hand under it. Then Reece was at her side. "Here," he ordered, "let me see."

"It's nothing!"

He took her by the wrist, putting the plug in the sink with his free hand. "You haven't broken the skin—you're better off immersing it in cold water."

The cold water did relieve the pain. Biting her lip, Lauren said, "There's a moral here—I shouldn't start fights before I've had my caffeine fix."

"You're still in love with Sandor."

Her wrist jerked in his hold like a trapped bird. "It was over years ago, Reece."

"Which isn't an answer—as you well know."

"You're not getting any other."

He moved closer to her, his eyes roaming her face. "No makeup," he said. "The real Lauren Courtney."

"You're unshaven," she responded in a flash, "but do you ever show the real Reece Callahan?"

With sudden deep bitterness he said, "Is there a real Reece Callahan?"

Shocked, she whispered, "If you have to ask the question, then of course there is."

"Oh, sure," he said, moving away from her and drying his hands. "Let's scrap this conversation. Did you say you wanted some toast?"

"Yes, please." Only wanting to lighten the atmosphere, she added, "This is a very intimidating kitchen—I'm what you might call an erratic cook."

He didn't smile. "Pull up a stool and I'll bring you a coffee. Cream and sugar?"

"No cream. Three spoonfuls of sugar."

"To sweeten you?"

"To kickstart the day. Creativity is enhanced by glucose—at least, that's my theory."

He gave his papers a disparaging glance. "With the negotiations I've got the next few days, maybe I should try it."

"Honey's better than sugar, and maple syrup's best of all."

"So you're a connoisseur of the creative process. You

should write a book,'' he said dryly, putting her coffee in front of her.

"No time... Do you know what, Reece? We've just had a real conversation. Our first."

"Don't push your luck," he rasped, "and don't see me as a challenge."

She flushed. "A useless venture?"

"Right on."

She said deliberately, "I don't believe you bought every one of the paintings and sculptures in this condo strictly as an investment."

"You can't take a hint, can you?" Reece said unpleasantly, taking the bread out of the toaster.

"The Madonna and child? An investment? You bought that statue because in some way it spoke to your heart."

His back was turned to her; briefly, his body shuddered as though she'd physically struck him. Then he pivoted, closing the distance between them in two quick strides. Towering over her, he dug his fingers into her shoulders. "Stay out of my private life, Lauren. I mean that!"

His eyes were blazing with emotion, a deep, vibrant blue; his face was so close to hers that she could see a small white scar on one eyelid. She'd hit home; she knew it. And found herself longing to take his face between her palms and comfort him.

He'd make burnt toast out of her if she tried. Swallowing hard, Lauren said with total truth, "I'm sorry—I didn't mean to hurt you."

He said harshly, "I'm going to be late for work. If your hand needs attention, the first-aid kit's in my bathroom cabinet. I'll see you this evening." Gathering all his papers in a bundle, he left the kitchen.

Thoughtfully Lauren started to eat her toast. The ice in his eyes had melted with a vengeance. And he'd bought the Madonna and child for intensely personal reasons that she was quite sure he had no intention of divulging.

One thing she knew. She wasn't going to be bored during the next few days.

CHAPTER FOUR

"LAUREN, what in hell are you doing?"

The chisel slipped, gouging into the wood. With an exclamation of chagrin, Lauren whirled around. "Don't ever creep up on me again when I'm working, Reece—look what you made me do! And what are you doing home anyway? You said six o'clock this evening."

Reece hauled his tie from around his throat. "It's six thirty-five and we're supposed to leave in twenty minutes."

Lauren's jaw dropped. "It can't be. I stopped for lunch no time ago."

"Six thirty-six," he said, ostentatiously looking at his gold watch.

"Oh, no," she wailed, "I promised I'd be ready."

"You did."

"Reece, I'm sorry. You'd better get out of here so I can change. I swear I won't be more than ten minutes late."

"What did you do to your finger?"

She glanced down at two Band-Aids adorning her index finger. "I cut it. No big deal."

"You're a mess," he said.

She looked down at herself, laughter flickering across her features. She was wearing her oldest leggings and a T-shirt embellished with several holes from her welding torch; her hair was pulled back into an untidy bundle on her neck. "You mean you won't take me to the cocktail party like this? Where's your sense of adventure?"

"I'm starting to wonder," Reece said with a note in his voice that brought her head up fast.

The words came from nowhere. "Don't you go seeing me as a challenge, either," she said.

"I'm beginning to think Wallace Harvarson has a lot more to answer for than a mere five hundred thousand dollars," he said tightly. "Go get ready, Lauren. Pin your hair up. Pile on the red nail polish. But for Pete's sake, hurry."

She started to laugh. "It'll take more than a few pins to make me presentable," she said, and stood up, moving away from the table and stretching her muscles with un-selfconscious grace.

The answering laughter vanished from Reece's face. He said sharply, "You did that today?" She nodded, watching him walk closer to the rough carving she'd been working on for the last few hours. He said, as though the words were being dragged from him, "I can see where you're headed—and already it's a thing of beauty."

"I thought I could just make a copy," Lauren said rue-fully, pulling the ribbon from her hair and shaking it in a cloud around her head. "But it got away from me."

The lines of the emerging sculpture of a mother and child were utterly modernistic, yet imbued with an ancient and ageless tenderness. Reece said in a hard voice, "I'm going to have a shower. I'll wait for you in the living room. I'm the host of this shindig this evening and I want to arrive on time."

"Yes, sir," she retorted, and watched him march across the dark-stained floors and out of the door. She put her chisel down on the table. Had she ever met a man who was such a mass of contradictions? He'd seen instantly what she was striving to create from the block of wood;

and run from it as though all the demons in hell were after him.

But she mustn't see him as a challenge.

The challenge, she thought wryly, looking down at herself, was to transform herself from a frump to a fashion model in less than twenty minutes. Move it, Lauren. You've got all week to figure out Reece Callahan.

It might take a lifetime. A thought she hastily subdued.

Seven o'clock. Lauren was late. Scowling, Reece switched to the news channel, and not for the first time wondered what in God's name had possessed him to suggest that Lauren Courtney pose as his lover. As a result, Wallace Harvarson was getting off scot-free and he, Reece, was saddled with an argumentative and thoroughly irritating woman who didn't count punctuality among her talents. Because she had talents. That bloody statue had got him by the throat the minute he'd seen it; which she, of course, had noticed right away.

The new federal budget was due to be tabled; he tried to pay attention. Then, behind him, overriding the newscaster's voice, he heard Lauren say, "Will I do?"

He flicked the remote control and stood up, turning to face her. She had draped herself against the door frame, her eyelids lowered demurely. Her dress was black, a full-length sheath slit to mid-thigh. A vivid scarlet-and-blue scarf swathed her throat and fell provocatively over one breast; her thin-strapped sandals had stiletto heels and her earrings dangled almost to her shoulders, little enameled discs of blue and red that moved with her breathing.

He said ironically, "You'll be noticed."

She smiled; her lips were also scarlet, he noticed, dry-mouthed. "Isn't that the whole aim?"

"I guess so." He walked closer, noticing her incredibly

long lashes. "How do you keep your hair up? It's contradicting all the laws of gravity."

It was piled in a mass of curls, making her neck look impossibly long and slender. "Pins and prayer," said Lauren.

"Let me see your hands."

"You would ask that," she said, and held them out, palms down. The hot coffee had left red blotches on the back of her left hand; she had two clean Band-Aids wrapped around her index finger.

"Do you often cut yourself?" he rapped.

"It's an occupational hazard," she said limpidly. "To quote you."

"Is the cut deep?"

"Nope. But I'm human. I bleed."

"In contrast to me."

"You said it. I didn't."

"You don't have to." He didn't know which he hated more, the way the black fabric clung to her breasts, or the mockery in her turquoise eyes. In a hard voice he added, "This is all very amusing and I'm sure we could stand here trading insults for the next hour. But my car's waiting downstairs. Let's go...and Lauren, don't forget what this is all about, will you? Wallace—remember him?"

"Are you telling me to behave myself?"

"Yeah. That's exactly what I'm doing."

"You don't have a worry in the world," she snapped. "I promise I'll be the perfect mistress."

She looked as though she'd rather take a chisel to him. A blunt chisel. He checked that he had his keys in the pocket of his tuxedo and said with a mockery equal to hers, "Shall we go, darling?"

Her nostrils flared. "If you think I'm going to start this charade one minute before I have to, you're out to lunch."

The sudden mad urge to take her in his arms and kiss her into submission surged through Reece's body with all the force and inevitability of an ocean wave. Oh, no, he thought, I'm not going there. Not with Lauren Courtney. Sure recipe for disaster. He said coldly, "I don't give a damn what you do when we're alone. But you'd better stick to the bargain in public. Or else the deal's off."

"Fine," she said. "Let's go."

She stalked to the elevator ahead of him, and stared at the control panel all the way down. His car was a black Porsche; he held the door while she folded herself into the passenger seat, revealing rather a lot of leg as she did so. Her silk stockings were black, her legs long and slender; his hormones in an uproar, Reece got into the driver's seat and slammed the door. Once this week was over, he'd find himself a woman. An agreeable woman without an artistic bone in her body. He'd been too long without one, that was his problem.

Nothing to do with Lauren.

In a silence that seethed with things unsaid, they drove to the city's most luxurious hotel. Reece pulled up in front of it. "Okay," he said, "we're on. You'd better act your little head off, sweetheart, or I'll pull the plug on your precious stepfather so fast you won't know what hit you."

"How nice," Lauren said, "an ultimatum. Guaranteed to make me feel as though we've been making mad, passionate love the whole day long."

Very deliberately he put his arm around her shoulders, caressing her bare flesh and dropping his head to run his lips along her throat. "We made mad, passionate love the minute I came home from work, that's why we're late…and we're going to do the same as soon as we get rid of all these people. Right, my darling?"

He felt her swallow against his cheek. "Right," she cooed and delicately nibbled at his ear with her teeth.

Sensation scorched along every nerve he possessed. The soft weight of her breast was pressed against his sleeve; her perfume, as sensual and complex as the woman herself, drifted to his nostrils. His body's response was instant and unequivocal. He wanted her. Wanted her in his bed. Now. Naked, beautiful and willing.

Then Lauren murmured against his earlobe, "You'd better not kiss me, not unless you want scarlet lipstick all over your face when we walk through the door. We don't have to be quite that convincing, do we?"

She was totally in control. That was the message. She didn't want him, Reece thought grimly. She was only toying with him, playing a role, the very role he'd insisted on.

He was an idiot. A prize jerk.

With a superhuman effort, he managed to say lazily, "I'm sure we can convince them we're mad for each other without the benefit of Revlon. Perhaps you'd better wipe my ear."

Her fingers were warm, brushing against his hair as they smoothed his flesh. He fought down a tide of sensation that would drown him if he let it and said, "The valet'll park the car. Let's go, Lauren."

She took his face between her palms, looked straight into his eyes and whispered with passionate intensity, "I'm crazy about you, honey. You know that, don't you?"

For a split second he found himself believing her, so convincing was the blaze of emotion in her eyes. But she was acting. Only acting. Feeling a rage as fierce as it was irrational clamp itself around his throat, he said, "Haven't I believed every word you've said from the moment we met?"

Her lashes flickered. Gotcha, he thought. "And don't call me honey. Even in jest." Then he climbed out of his car, passing the keys to the uniformed valet. "Callahan's the name," he told him easily.

"Thank you, sir."

Reece walked to Lauren's door, opened it, and took her hand, raising it to his lips. "Have I told you yet how beautiful you look?"

She swayed toward him, her lips in a provocative pout. "A hundred times and never enough."

A man's voice said loudly, "Reece—good to see you."

Reece turned. "Marcus, I'm glad you could make it. And Tiffany, how nice to see you. May I introduce Lauren Courtney? Dearest, this is Marcus Wheelwright, CEO of the European branch of my company...and his daughter Tiffany."

Marcus was fiftyish, heavy-set and jovial. Tiffany, Reece noticed, was her usual ice-maiden self, wearing a white satin gown with diamonds glittering around her throat, her blond hair sleekly perfect. He wouldn't be surprised if Lauren's hairdo fell down before the night was over; but Tiffany's would never do that. And Tiffany was probably never late for anything. Hurriedly he brought his attention back as Marcus shook Lauren's hand. "Not the sculptor?" Marcus asked. "I didn't know you two knew each other."

"We met recently," Reece said. "Love at first sight, wasn't it, darling?"

Lauren laughed up at him, lacing her arm through his. "Absolutely...I'm still in a state of shock. Are you based in Paris, Marcus?"

"Paris. Hamburg. Oslo. You name it," Marcus said; he had the look of a man recovering from a disagreeable revelation. Whereas Tiffany, Reece noticed, looked coldly furious.

Lauren started to discuss the art market in Paris, skillfully including Tiffany and Reece in the conversation, every movement of her body giving out the message that she was a satiated woman who'd been equally generous in return. It was a masterful performance, Reece thought savagely, and struggled to play his part. Then Marcus drew him aside with a question about their French office; answering automatically, all his senses keyed to Lauren, Reece heard Tiffany say, "So you're Reece's latest plaything."

"That's not what I would have called myself," Lauren replied.

"Don't fool yourself on that count—I'm the one who'll last. I have breeding, all the right connections." Tiffany gave Lauren's earrings a scornful glance. "And taste."

"Whereas I'm merely talented, intelligent and beautiful," Lauren said.

"Also incredibly conceited!"

"Merely realistic."

Reece smothered the urge to laugh out loud and tried to pay attention to Marcus, who wanted to fire his office manager; deflecting him from the topic, Reece said heartily, "I should go inside, Marcus. I'm glad you and Tiffany have had the chance to meet Lauren—I'm a very lucky guy."

"You certainly are," Lauren said, laughing as she briefly laid her head on his shoulder; several of her curls, he noticed, were already tumbling from their pins. He let his palm rest warm on her nape, feeling the contact scour his nerves in a way that had nothing to do with deception and everything to do with his hormones. He didn't need to act. He lusted after Lauren Courtney like a tomcat in springtime.

Did he want her to know that?

He did not.

"I'll talk to you later," he said to Marcus and Tiffany. "Come along, darling, let's get a drink."

As he and Lauren walked arm in arm into the glittering ballroom, decorated with tall standards of lilies and thousands of tiny gold lights, she said sweetly, "I don't know why you want to discourage Tiffany. She's perfect for you—there's ice in her veins, too."

"You wouldn't by any chance be daring me to prove otherwise?"

"No! I'm simply making an observation."

"I'm not so sure about that. Are you forgetting that once midnight rolls around, you and I will be alone in my condo?"

Her arm tensed under his. "But you promised—"

"Ah...there's Cindy," he said casually. "If you can get past her, you can deceive anyone."

Cindy Lothan, the wife of another of his CEO's, had a brain like a steel trap; she and her husband made a formidable pair. Swiftly Reece made the introductions. But Lauren was relaxed and charming, drawing Cindy out with a skill Reece had to admire. As Lauren discussed the latest upsets in the stock market with every air of knowing what she was talking about, he put his arm around her waist, caressing the swell of her hip. She quivered in response like a high-strung racehorse. Reece's thrill of primitive triumph just as quickly turned to ashes in his mouth. She was acting. Only acting. And he'd damn well better remember it.

Lauren always at his side, Reece played the room, making the contacts he needed to make, saying what he needed to say. The dinner was delicious, his speech went extremely well, and he danced almost exclusively with Lauren, fighting with all his willpower to control his body's response to her closeness. By the time midnight rolled around, he felt as though the evening had lasted for three days. He looped his arm around Lauren's shoulders and said with intimate ease, "Sweetheart, I think we should head home—are you ready?"

Her lips curved in a smile laced with sexual complicity. "I thought you'd never ask."

To hell with this, Reece decided, and for a moment allowed his very real desire to blaze from his eyes; and watched her own eyes widen and color rise in her cheeks. The room fell away. She can't be acting now, he thought. No one could make herself blush to order. Not even Lauren.

He said huskily, "I want to be alone with you."

Her tongue traced the softness of her lower lip. "And I with you."

What he really wanted was to tear her dress from her body and make love to her on the hotel carpet. Forcing himself to smother the image of her naked limbs sprawled in graceful abandon at his feet, he said roughly, "Let's go, then."

However, everyone they passed wanted to say goodnight and thank him for a great party, conversations from which Reece extricated himself with rather less than his usual expertise. But finally they made it to the lobby and the valet disappeared to get his car. Lauren slipped into the passenger seat, Reece put his foot to the accelerator and they surged away from the hotel.

Lauren said flatly, "Thank God that's over. I don't think I've ever worked so hard in all my life."

It was as though she'd flung cold water in his face. So

she'd been acting all along, he thought furiously. Right down to the blush. He said in a voice from which he removed any trace of emotion, "You did a fine job. Deception comes easy to you."

She shot him an unfriendly look. "You're no slouch in that department yourself."

"Isn't corporate ethics considered a contradiction in terms? As opposed to artistic integrity, that is?"

"You're spoiling for a fight, aren't you?" she fumed. "I'm only too happy to oblige. Every person in that hotel ballroom thinks you and I are having a scorcher of an affair. And when I disappear from your life next week, they'll assume you dumped me. Because, of course, no woman in her right mind would give up the opportunity to get her greedy little paws on your millions."

"On day eight," Reece snarled, "we'll stage the granddaddy of all rows plunk in the middle of the Vancouver airport, and you can tell me to go to hell. You can shout it from the bloody rooftops as far as I care. The fight at least won't be acting and the press can have a field day with me being the dumpee rather than the dumper."

He pulled up with a jerk at a red light. Lauren said in an odd voice, "But you hate gossip."

"Not as much as I hate acting," Reece declared, and wondered what on earth had possessed him to say that.

He glanced over at her. She no longer looked angry. Instead she was staring down at her hands, which were linked in her lap. In a small voice she said, "You weren't acting some of the time. Are you going to leap on me as soon as we get to your place? Because if so, I'll get out now and go to a hotel."

Rather a lot of her hair had tumbled down her neck; she looked tired and unhappy. He quelled an uprush of compassion, saying coldly, "You dress in slinky black crepe, fall all over me and expect me to behave like that chunk of wood you're carving? I'm a normal red-blooded male, for Pete's sake.''

"And I'm passably pretty.''

So she'd noticed that particular deception. "I take that back. You really are the most beautiful woman I've ever seen.''

"Oh, sure.''

"It's the truth!''

Her head jerked up; he noticed with another of those disconcerting surges of emotion that she'd chewed some of the lipstick from her bottom lip. "You know what?'' she declaimed. "I don't have a clue when you're telling the truth and when you're lying yourself blue in the face.''

The lights changed. He drove across the junction and said impatiently, "You think I've got you all figured out?''

She sighed. "I suppose it doesn't really matter, does it? This is only about acting, and there's only a week to go. But you haven't answered the question. Are you going to leap on me, Reece?''

"No.''

Her fingers were still twisting in her lap. "Can I trust you?''

He said with cold fury, "I'm not into rape.''

"At least admit that I'm smart to be asking the question.''

His own anger died. "I'm six inches taller than you and eighty pounds heavier. Yeah, you're right.''

A faint smile lit up her face. "Thanks.''

It wasn't part of the next seven days for him to start liking her. "Ten minutes and we'll be home,'' he said repressively.

"You'll be home—I won't.''

"Give it a rest, Lauren.''

Conspicuously she said not one more word, gazing out of the window as they drove toward the park. As Reece pulled up outside his condo, he said, "Try not to look as though you hate my guts in front of the doorman, okay?"

Her eyes glittering, she said, "But, honeybunch, your body drives me mad. Surely that includes your guts."

He wanted to laugh at her audacity; he wanted to kiss her senseless. He did neither. Rather, he walked around the hood of his car, helped Lauren out with the air of a man who had seduction on his mind, and, his arm snug around her waist, said good-night to the doorman. The elevator door opened and closed behind them. Reece dropped his arm, moved away from her and said in a clipped voice, "Tomorrow night is a private dinner party in Shaughnessy Heights. Three other couples. I'm wearing a business suit. Be ready by seven."

"I'll set the beeper on my watch to go off at six," Lauren said with equal crispness. "That way I won't forget."

He was easily forgettable. That was the message. Swiftly Reece unlocked the door of his condo and stood back for her to precede him. She said, her back to him, "I'll see you tomorrow."

"Sweet dreams," he said ironically, and watched her hurry across the living room with none of her usual grace. He then stripped off his tie, poured himself a stiff whiskey and flipped on the television movie channel. Comedy. Drama. Violence. It didn't matter. Anything to distract him from Lauren's body and his ferocious need to possess that body.

What he mustn't forget was what a consummate actress she was.

CHAPTER FIVE

THE following evening Lauren marched into the living room of Reece's condo at ten to seven. Tonight it was Reece who was going to be late, she thought irritably, and tried to focus on a delightful Chardin oil painting hanging beside a Stieglitz photograph.

The key clicked in the lock and Reece walked in, hauling at his tie and flinging his jacket on the nearest chair. Then he saw her and for a moment stopped dead. "You're on time."

"I'm not always late."

"But you're always argumentative... I'm going to have a shower. Ten minutes. Help yourself to a drink."

She didn't need a drink. She needed to stay stone cold sober the entire evening. She picked up the small sketch pad she'd brought from her room and started copying a Picasso stroke for stroke. Reece Callahan was nothing to her. Nothing.

If Wallace were alive, he should be down on his knees to her in gratitude.

If Wallace were alive, she wouldn't be here.

Her sketch was a disaster and her fingers were cold. She tossed the pad on a wing chair and went to stand by the window, blind to the panoramic view of Stanley Park and the snowcapped Rockies. Then Reece came back in the room. He was fiddling with a gold cuff link, his shoulders very broad in his pristine white shirt, his damp hair curling over his ears.

"My turn to be late tomorrow night," Lauren said.

"You've got the night off tomorrow—I fly to Seattle for meetings and won't be home until nine or so."

She didn't try to mask her relief. Reece said curtly, "The following morning we leave for Whistler. Don't wear an outfit like that for the Japanese delegation."

Don't tell me what to do, she thought. "You don't like what I'm wearing?" she purred, fluttering her lashes at him. "But you bought it for me, remember? You said you couldn't wait to get me home and tear it from my body."

"If the market ever dries up for bronze sculptures, you could make B-grade movies," Reece jeered. "Let's go. Our host's name is Brian, his wife's Bianca, and she's the one who's out to get me."

"No accounting for taste," Lauren remarked, and picked up her black wool shawl from the chair, throwing it around her shoulders.

"Smart move, wearing that shawl," Reece said, ushering her out the door. "So you won't catch pneumonia."

Her jade-green top did show rather a lot of cleavage. Her wide-legged silk pants swishing softly as she walked toward the elevator, Lauren said amiably, "If you've got it, flaunt it, and the level of this conversation is definitely B-grade."

He pushed the button for the ground floor; then his gaze wandered to the creamy curves of her collarbone, and the shadow between her breasts. "Oh, you've got it."

Color crept up Lauren's cheeks. She'd worn this outfit before and thought nothing of it. Why should Reece Callahan make her feel as shy and uncertain as an adolescent? She found herself longing for the evening to be over before it had even begun; to be alone in her bedroom, away from a man who unsettled and infuriated her. Then Reece took her by the shoulders, his lips drifting down her throat to the hollow at its base. Her pulse leaped, then began to race with frantic speed. The elevator doors opened.

She said in a venomous whisper, "The doorman's nowhere in sight. You can quit right away."

Against her skin he murmured, "Security cameras—this is for their benefit."

The waft of his breath jangled every nerve she possessed. She lifted her fingers to stroke his thick dark hair, discovering it to be unexpectedly silky to the touch, and said shakily, "Darling, we're already late."

As he moved away from her, his arm brushed the fullness of her breast; her indrawn breath was no act, Lauren realized with a lurch of her heart, and felt her nipples harden. Hurriedly she drew the shawl around her body and almost ran outside to Reece's car. How could her body betray her by responding to a man she both disliked and feared?

Frigid was a word Sandor had thrown at her more than once during their stormy relationship; in the ensuing months and years, not one of the men she'd dated had tempted her to have an affair. Her conclusion had been inevitable: sex wasn't for her.

Not that she was contemplating having sex with Reece. That was out of the question.

"You're very quiet," Reece said, starting the car.

She shivered. "There's no audience."

"Are you cold?"

She huddled into her shawl. "No. Thanks."

"Sometimes you behave like a Victorian virgin," he said, whipping out into the traffic. "And how's that for a laugh?"

Ridiculously, Lauren felt tears prickle at the backs of her eyes. But she never cried, and she wasn't going to start with Reece Callahan. She said with sudden fierce honesty,

"I'm so tired of all the innuendoes and sneers from men who believed Sandor's version of events without even asking me if I had a different version. You're just like them, Reece—I'm condemned before I even walk in the room. Not that I give a hoot in hell what you think about me...and that's the last word you're getting out of me until we arrive." Ostentatiously turning her face to the window, she closed her eyes.

She didn't fall asleep, she was too riled up for that. But she didn't cry, either. When eventually they pulled into a long curve of driveway, Reece said evenly, "We're here."

Lauren sat up, opened her purse and checked her lipstick. "I'll do the best I can this evening because of Wallace. Just don't forget it's an act, will you?"

He said with dangerous softness, "Lauren, when I kissed your throat, I felt your pulse race. That wasn't an act."

"More proof that I'm easy—that Sandor's right," she said bitterly, and climbed out of the car. A Tudor mansion loomed in the darkness; she disliked it on sight, and stalked toward the huge oak door with its insets of mullioned glass. Fake beams, fake glass and fake woman, she thought, and rounded on Reece, her eyes glittering. "You know what? I hate the sight of you."

His answer was to bury his hands in her tumble of loose curls and kiss her hard on the mouth. As the front door opened, Reece released her so quickly that she staggered, turning a stunned face to her host. She said weakly, "You must be Brian," and held out her hand. It was, she noticed, trembling slightly.

With a courtesy she had to admire, Brian ignored her confusion. "Hello, Lauren, welcome to Stratford House...Reece, come in. Oh, here's Bianca. Darling, this is Reece's friend, Lauren Courtney. You're from Manhattan, am I right, Lauren?''

Bianca was a voluptuous brunette who looked ready to throttle her, Lauren thought with distant humor. Bianca must have seen that kiss on the front step: a kiss from which Lauren was still inwardly reeling. It had been so sudden and so shocking that she'd had no time to react. Wasn't this even more proof that all those horrible accusations Sandor had hurled at her were still true? Frigid. Ungenerous. Heartless. On and on they'd gone, and she in her vulnerability had believed him.

Desperately she tried to pull herself together, praying Reece was in ignorance of her response. Or rather, her lack of it. Because, of course, he'd kissed her hoping Bianca would see. All part of the act.

With a superhuman effort Lauren managed to sound relaxed. "I'm so pleased to meet you, Bianca."

"Do come in," Bianca said with minimal warmth. Then, her voice changing, she added, "How are you, Reece? Lovely to see you. Let me get you a drink while Brian introduces Lauren to our other guests."

Divide and conquer, Lauren thought shrewdly, and tucked her arm into Reece's. "I'm actually rather thirsty, Bianca. We had to rush around so we wouldn't be late, didn't we, darling?" she said, smiling besottedly up at Reece.

There were sparks of blue fire in his eyes as he lifted her fingers to his lips, kissing her knuckles with lingering pleasure. "Until I met you, I was known as Mr. Punctuality," he said. "Right, Brian? Lead the way, Bianca. I'll introduce Lauren to the rest in a few minutes."

Lauren knew she was blushing. All the better, she thought wildly. It adds veracity. And I'll make darn sure Bianca doesn't put arsenic in my wine.

As they followed Bianca into a paneled library where an imposing oak bar and a great many horse brasses took precedence over the books, Reece winked at her. Impulsively she winked back, bumping him gently with her hip and watching his irises darken. His strongly carved lips curled in a smile; his eyes weren't at all like ice. Was it act or reality? Desire or deception?

Did she really want the answers?

With all the social ease and charm she was capable of, she engaged Bianca in conversation. When they went into a living room dominated by overstuffed furniture, she kept her arm tucked into Reece's and interspersed her remarks with adoring looks and endearments. What did it matter that the other guests would label her a clinging vine? That was the deal she'd struck.

The food was excellent, the wine flowed freely, and the conversation sparkled. Lauren was seated across from Reece. As she took the last spoonful of raspberry torte, she glanced over at him. He was laughing at something Brian had said, and as though she'd never seen him before, his image imprinted itself on her mind: his white teeth and tanned face, alive with strength and intelligence; the lock of dark hair falling on his forehead; the entirely masculine vitality that infused every one of his movements. Handsome, sexy, and utterly male. How could she ever have thought him a cold fish?

He spells danger, she thought blankly. Maybe the reason she hadn't really looked at him before had been pure self-protection. Because if she'd looked, she'd never have embarked on this crazy scheme.

Six more days. She'd be all right. Of course she would.

The party broke up at one a.m., Reece and Lauren being the last to leave. Again Lauren did her imitation of a clinging vine, neatly foiling Bianca's attempt to corral Reece and show him the new solarium. As soon as they were in his car with the doors shut, she announced, "You owe me, buddy. Big time."

He laughed, putting the key in the ignition. "Did you ever play interference in football? You'd be a natural."

"You're the one built like a football player," she said incautiously.

"Don't tell me that's a compliment?"

She'd drunk rather too much Cabernet Sauvignon and in the semidarkness she didn't feel the slightest bit frigid. "I believe it is," she said. "Imagine that."

"Seriously, Lauren, you did wonders this evening. You kept Bianca from eating me alive and no one else even realized what was going on. Thanks."

"Beyond the call of duty?" she said with a cheeky grin, and slid her feet out of her elegant pumps with a sigh of relief. "That's better—my feet are killing me. I've been scared to take my shoes off at dinner parties ever since someone swiped my shoes during the speeches at a reception I once went to. I had to walk out in my stockinged feet with my nose in the air, as though it was the latest fashion to go unshod to fancy parties."

Reece threw back his head, laughing all the way from his belly. "I promise I'll always protect you from shoe thieves, my darling Lauren."

My darling Lauren... Lauren said primly, "That's very nice of you, Reece."

Still chuckling, he began asking her about the reception. From there they moved to a Broadway play they'd both seen, and before she knew it, they were back at the condo. Reece opened the car door on her side. Then he leaned over and picked her up, straightening and heading for the lobby. "Put me down," Lauren croaked.

"Your feet are hurting. It's the least I can do after

Bianca,'' he said, and smiled at the doorman. The elevator doors opened and shut. In its gleaming gold walls, Lauren gazed at the outline of a tall dark-clad man holding a woman whose hair rippled over his sleeve, and felt herself tremble with what was surely desire.

Desire? Her?

I don't desire him, she thought frantically. I can't! This is a business arrangement, it's only going to last a few more days. I mustn't get involved. Anyway, I hate sex. Sandor saw to that.

She wriggled in Reece's arms. ''You can put me down now. No one's watching.''

He tightened his hold. ''This is nothing to do with the doorman,'' he said, carrying her out of the elevator and along the thick carpet. Stooping slightly, he inserted the key in the lock and then kicked the door shut behind him. ''Stop squirming,'' he said thickly, ''it's driving me nuts.''

She squirmed all the harder. ''Reece, put me down!''

Swiftly he lowered her to the floor, put his arms around her and kissed her with a fierce possessiveness.

Lauren stood stiff as a china doll in his arms. For the second time Reece was kissing her. But this time there was no Bianca to impress; only the two of them in an empty apartment. This time he wasn't acting. Fear flicked her nerves sharp as a whip, memories surging back of what it had been like with Sandor, that long-ago sensation of being smothered by his weight, by the power he had wielded over her.

But then, as though a pendulum had swung from one extreme to the other, fear was usurped by a flood of other sensations. The warmth of Reece's lips, so confident of their welcome. The slide of his palms down her back to her waist, the hard wall of his chest pressing against her breasts. Her blood started thrumming in her veins and an ache of desire—unquestionably it was desire—blossomed in her belly. In sheer surprise her body sagged in Reece's embrace. Without even considering what she was doing, Lauren clutched the sleeves of his jacket and kissed him back; and wondered if she could faint from sheer pleasure.

His lips teased hers apart. She felt the first thrust of his tongue and welcomed it with all her heart, her hands moving to his shoulders, then linking themselves at his nape, where his hair brushed her skin with tantalizing softness.

His kiss deepened, an intimacy she was more than ready for, her body melting into his. His arms tightened around her waist, his fingers digging into the curve of her hip. With one hand he found the swell of her breast, caressing its firm rise with lingering sensitivity. Lauren gave a tiny, spontaneous cry of delight. He said huskily, against her mouth, "My beautiful Lauren..." Then, again, he swept her up into his arms.

Through eyes dazzled with longing, she realized he was carrying her across the room, past the Picasso and the Chardin to the doorway of his bedroom. He pushed the door open with his foot, and once again she saw the wonderful bronze sculpture against the forest-green wall, and the shimmering lights of the park beyond the balcony. The bed looked huge, and it was this that finally made Lauren find her voice. "Reece, what's going on? I—"

He lowered her to the floor so that she was enclosed in his embrace, and said hoarsely, "You're where you belong."

"But we—"

He closed her mouth with his own, and in a surge of sweetness she forgot about Sandor's cruelty. Had she ever in her life felt so encompassed by a man's embrace? So certain that it was here in Reece's bedroom that she did indeed belong? Knowing she was taking a huge step into the unknown, Lauren wrapped her arms around his waist, her palms seeking the warmth of his skin beneath his shirt. His muscles were tense, the hard curves of his rib cage exciting her beyond measure. Of their own volition her hands smoothed his chest and the taut, rippled belly, and all the while his tongue played with hers in a heated kiss she wanted to last forever.

Against her mouth, he muttered, "I wanted you the first moment I saw you walk into my office—why else did I suggest this crazy arrangement of ours?"

Her body froze, desire obliterated with horrifying suddenness. Wrenching her head back, Lauren gasped, "But you believed Sandor then, you said so."

He nibbled at her lips, saying thickly, "This is no time for talking. I want to see you naked, I want to—"

"And now I'm proving you right, aren't I?" she gabbled. "I'm easy, I'm promiscuous, I've only known you for four days and I'm about to fall into your bed."

"For God's sake—you've had other lovers since Sandor, you must have."

"I haven't! I told you I hadn't."

"What does it matter?" Reece said impatiently, clasping her by the shoulders. "We're meant to be together, I know we are. Anything else is irrelevant."

Her heart now felt as though it was encased in ice. "You think it's irrelevant whether or not you believe me about something as basic as promiscuity?"

"If you've had other lovers, Lauren, that doesn't mean you're promiscuous."

"You don't believe one word I've said, do you?" she cried, pulling away from him. "How can that be irrelevant?"

He said harshly, "We're not marrying each other."

"No. Just having a one-night stand. Or a one-week

stand." She struggled to get her breath through the pain in her chest. "I must be mad to have kissed you—why did I do that?"

"Because you wanted to."

He was right. For the first time in many years, she'd craved a man's body, opened herself to his kisses and his touch without a thought for the consequences or the context: behavior so totally out of character that in the last few minutes she'd become a stranger to herself. And it was Reece who had done that to her. A man she scarcely knew, rich, ruthless, and full of secrets. Reece with his beautiful body and his implacable will.

He said grimly, "At least you're not bothering to deny it."

Swallowing hard, Lauren fought to find the words that might bring her back from the chasm into which she had so nearly tumbled. The simplest thing would be to turn tail and run for home as fast as she could; but if she did so, Wallace's good name would be ruined. She said with icy precision, "I'll function as a hostess for the Japanese wives—not as your mistress. The same goes for your contact at the yacht club. In other words, for the rest of our time together we can stop acting. And then I'm out of here. So fast you won't see me for the dust."

His eyes like shards of glass, Reece said, "You're burning your bridges, Lauren—I could be useful to you. I know a lot of people with the kind of money to afford your sculptures."

"As investments," she said bitterly. "No, thanks. I've made my own way in the world so far, and I'll continue to do so."

"With help from Sandor. And Wallace."

"That's right," she said furiously, "rub my nose in my mistakes. Of course, you never make them, do you?

You're not a fallible human being like the rest of us—I bet you've never done a single thing you've regretted with all your heart.''

His fingers bit into her flesh with cruel strength. "I told you to stay out of my personal life," he blazed. "But do you listen? You—"

"So you have made mistakes...big ones, by the look of you," she said in a dazed voice.

"I—"

"Won't you tell me about them?" she begged. "Please?"

"I will not—they're none of your goddamned business," he grated, pushing her away as though he couldn't bear to touch her, then wiping his palms down the sides of his trousers.

Cut to the quick, Lauren cried, "Thank God, I didn't get into your bed. The only thing you're willing to share is your body, isn't it, Reece? Go ahead and do that with other women if that's what turns you on. But I deserve more than that. I want a man who'll share himself body and soul." She bit her lip, wondering where her words had come from, certain in her heart they were true. "I'll be ready Tuesday morning to go to Whistler. In the meantime, I don't want to lay eyes on you."

"You'll stay here tonight and tomorrow night," he said in an ugly voice. "Or the deal's off."

"You're just like Sandor—in love with power," she retorted, too angry to care what she said. "So how could you ever fall in love with an ordinary person? A woman with feelings and integrity? I wouldn't make love with you if you were the last man on earth."

"Yes, you would," he sneered. "If I'd kept my mouth shut about wanting you in my office, you'd be in my bed right now. Because you were willing, Lauren—that was no act.''

She'd been more than willing: against all her experience and expectations, she'd been enraptured. Her shoulders slumping, she said wearily, "So you get the last word— good for you.''

As she turned away, Reece made no move to stop her. Feeling as though she'd been run over by a truck, Lauren trailed to her bedroom and shut the door, leaning back against the frame. All this luxury and elegance, yet she might as well be in prison.

There were only six more days left in her sentence. Six days and six nights.

It was the nights she had to worry about. Because Reece had been right: she would have made love with him. Just as if Sandor hadn't time and time again convinced her she was a wipeout in bed, a failure as a woman.

But she'd learned her lesson. She wouldn't lay as much as a finger on Reece from now on.

She couldn't afford to. Not when acting could so easily turn into reality.

CHAPTER SIX

LAUREN worked like a woman possessed all the next day, and by seven that evening knew she had to stop. The carving of mother and child was as complete as she could make it; now she had to put it away for a month and then look at it afresh to see if it had accomplished what she'd hoped for.

She was almost sure it had: that it was both powerful and true. Carefully she draped it in one of the towels from the bathroom. As always when she'd finished a piece, she felt drained yet restless, too wound up to settle to anything, too wired to sleep. One thing she knew: she'd prefer not to be in the condo when Reece returned from Seattle.

On impulse she phoned Charlie. "It's Lauren. Any chance you're free for a visit?"

"I'd love to see you. I haven't eaten yet—feel like Szechuan food?"

That's just what Lauren needed: a crowded restaurant and some good food. "Great idea!" They agreed to meet in Chinatown, and Lauren went to have a shower. An hour later, she and Charlie were seated across from each other in a dimly lit restaurant decorated with red dragons and tasseled lights, sipping Chinese tea and eating meat dumplings in a ferociously spicy sauce.

Charlie said briskly, "Okay, Lauren, come clean. What's it like being the mistress of the richest man in town?"

"I'm not!"

"So you've come close," Charlie said shrewdly. "I'm not surprised—I figured there was dynamite somewhere in

Reece Callahan. You don't get where he is without having all kinds of drive and a killer instinct.''

"He's an arrogant, hard-nosed tyrant who doesn't know the difference between the truth and a lie. Especially if a woman's doing the talking.''

Charlie grimaced. "So he believes Sandor's version of your past and he's blind to what's under his nose?''

"Precisely.'' Lauren swallowed too much sauce and nearly choked. Hastily she gulped some tea. "But it really doesn't matter. Five more days and I'm home free.''

"It matters. By the look of you.''

Charlie was an old and trusted friend. Lauren said flatly, "Can you believe he turns me on? What's *wrong* with me?''

"I told you he was a hunk.''

"I get the occasional glimpse that there's a real human being buried inside him—and then he does something that makes me so angry I could spit.''

Heartlessly Charlie began to laugh. "About time you paid some attention to the opposite sex.''

"I've never stopped dating,'' Lauren said indignantly.

"Safe men. Predictable men. How long since you've been with a man who infuriates you and yet you want to jump his bones?''

Lauren said in a staccato voice, "I will not jump Reece Callahan's bones or any other part of his anatomy.''

"What would be the harm if you did?''

"I might find out I liked it,'' Lauren blurted, then pulled a face of sheer horror. "Can you believe I just said that?''

"I can and you did.''

"And where would it get me, to have an affair with Reece? After next Saturday we go our separate ways.''

Her expression suddenly serious, Charlie rested a hand on Lauren's wrist. "Maybe you should go for it anyway.

It's time you got out of the prison Sandor built for you...you've let him run your life far too long. Sandor was a handsome, charming manipulator with an ego as big as an oil tanker and not a shred of human kindness...you deserve better than to trail in his wake for the rest of your life."

"Your description of Sandor would apply equally well to Reece Callahan," Lauren said tartly.

"They're as different as night and day—and you know it."

"So Reece is better looking."

"Sandor was hollow inside," Charlie announced. "Reece isn't. That's the difference."

"Huh," Lauren said, unconvinced. "The fact remains, I was taken in by Sandor, and I'm in no hurry to repeat my mistake."

"Of course you were taken in by him. He was your instructor, he was talented, sexy and charismatic. And you were very young when you first met him. Why wouldn't you be taken in?"

Lauren gave a deep sigh. "I'm afraid to trust my instincts anymore," she said unhappily. "Basically, I'm afraid to trust men. In case I get hurt again."

"But you take so many risks in your work. Couldn't you spread them out to include the men in your life?"

"Once I get back to New York, I might."

"You could start right here in Vancouver."

"Charlie, are you serious? Are you really advising me to have an affair with Reece?"

"Yep."

"Surefire recipe for disaster."

"You might indeed find out you like it."

It wasn't an opportune moment for Lauren to remember how her body had melted into Reece's, her lips parting to the thrust of his tongue. She took another gulp of tea, hoping her flushed cheeks could be attributed to the sauce. Charlie said smugly, "I rest my case."

"You don't miss a trick, do you? But how can a man I totally dislike have my hormones doing the hiphop?"

"Good question. By the time I've eaten my curried duck, maybe I can come up with an answer."

"I shouldn't have dumped all that garbage about Reece on you, Charlie—"

"It wasn't garbage and I think you should hang in there with him. I do trust my instincts, and they're telling me he's a very different ball game from Sandor."

"Maybe I'll try not to lose my temper so often," Lauren said thoughtfully, "that'd be a start." Then, reaching for the bill, she glanced down at her watch. "Eleven-ten?" she exclaimed. "It can't be!"

So it was nearly quarter to twelve by the time Lauren inserted her key into the lock of Reece's condo. Before she could fully turn it, the door was wrenched open. Reece said furiously, "Where the *hell* have you been?"

He was wearing jeans and an open-necked shirt; his hair was tousled and his eyes blazed blue. He was also, Lauren saw, white about the mouth. "Out with a friend," she said, puzzled. "What's the matter?"

He grabbed her by one arm and hauled her into the room. "For God's sake, are you okay? And where the devil *were* you?"

She didn't like being manhandled; never had since her days with Sandor. But remembering her resolve, Lauren said as calmly as she could, "I was having dinner in Chinatown."

"Why didn't you leave me a note telling me where you were?"

"Because it didn't occur to me," she said truthfully. "Let go of my arm."

"I didn't have a clue what you were up to!"

"Reece, I'm twenty-seven years old and you're not my keeper!"

"And who's this friend? What's *his* name?"

"It was a woman and what's it to you?"

"We're yelling at each other again," he said flatly. "Lauren, I genuinely thought you were in some kind of trouble."

His jawline was tight, and his shoulders still rigid with tension. "Trouble?" she repeated, frowning. "What kind of trouble?"

"This is a big city. Any number of things could have happened. So next time just leave me a note, will you?"

"I live in Manhattan—I'm streetwise. You don't have to worry about me."

"You're an extremely attractive woman who's carrying a purse with a wallet in it, and while this may not be New York, Vancouver's got its own share of criminals."

"So you can fly to Seattle but I'm supposed to sit home in your condo and wait for you to get back? You've got the wrong woman!"

"You think I don't know that?"

"Not for much longer, though. Whistler and the yacht club—then you can kiss me goodbye." Her sense of humor getting the better of her, she added, "Metaphorically, that is."

"Keep your metaphors," Reece said violently. "I want to kiss you right now and I mean that literally."

"Because I'm easy," she flashed.

"Because you make me say things I have no intention of saying. Because the sheen of your hair, the curve of your lips are driving me out of my mind. Because you've ambushed my orderly, very-much-under-my-control life. How's that for starters?''

"Oh," said Lauren.

He ran his fingers through his already disordered hair. "I was pretty sure you wouldn't abandon our agreement without letting me know—so I decided you were in some kind of trouble. But I had no idea where to start looking for you."

Something shifted deep within her. "You're saying you trust me? About the agreement?"

"You might drop it in the middle of one of our yelling matches," he said wryly. "But you wouldn't sneak off when I'm not here. Not your style."

"I would have been home earlier, but my friend and I got talking." Lauren added generously, "I'm sorry I worried you, Reece—that wasn't my intention."

He turned away, heading for the living room. "I need a drink," he said. "Want anything?"

"Sure, I'll have a glass of wine." Running her fingers absently over the copper sculpture, she said, "I still don't understand why you were so upset. It wasn't for the sake of my big blue eyes—so what else was going on?"

He passed her a crystal glass of Chardonnay, and took a healthy swallow from his whiskey. "Leave it, will you?"

"You sure know how to shut doors in people's faces."

"Talking of shut doors, I went into your room. Looking for you. The sculpture's beautiful, Lauren."

She didn't like the thought of him in her bedroom. But she'd already lost her temper once in the last five minutes and she wasn't going to do it again. "That was the main reason I had to go out...I'm always at a loose end when I finish a piece."

"So," said Reece, his eyes suddenly as intent as a hunter's, "where do we go from here?"

Her fingers tightened around her glass. "Whistler," she said fliply. "Where else?"

"I'm not talking geography."

"In that case, nowhere."

"We could go to bed. Now. Together."

Her heart gave an uncomfortable lurch. "No, Reece, I won't do that. We agreed to be lovers in public, not in private and we went through all this last night."

"You want to make love with me."

Only when you touch me. "It's been nearly four years, why wouldn't I?"

"You keep saying you haven't been to bed with anyone for four years—you really expect me to believe that?"

"Yes," she said, her chin raised, "I do."

He swished the amber liquid in his glass, his eyes never leaving her face. "In which case, the way you respond to me—I shouldn't take it personally. Anyone would do."

"*I* don't know," she cried. "I've dated men in the last four years and not one of them has tempted me to abandon celibacy. Not like you." She tossed back some wine. "And why am I telling you all this? The bottom line is that I'm not going to bed with you. And that's that."

He said disagreeably, "What are you holding out for?"

"You would think that!"

"Let's quit the playacting, okay? I want you in my bed. But I'm damned if I'll dress it up into something it's not."

"With adoring looks and endearments? The way we've been behaving in public?"

"Precisely."

"Reece," she said, "have you ever been in love?"

He scowled at her. "Not since I was sixteen and crazy about the girl next door."

"So as an adult you've never given yourself to a woman body and soul?"

"No. Of course I haven't."

Delicately she raised her brows. "Of course you haven't? Maybe you should try it sometime. It'd turn your controlled life upside down—I guarantee it."

Very deliberately, he ran his finger down the curve of her cheek to the corner of her mouth, watching her eyes dilate. "Sex between you and me would be passionate, inventive and powerful. But I'm not going to call it romance, and I'm not going to call it love."

"You're not going to call it anything. Because it isn't going to happen."

"I could persuade you."

She took an involuntary step backward. "How long since a woman said no to you? Too long. Obviously."

"If you think I'm going to beg, you've got it wrong."

Suddenly exhausted, her voice thin with strain, Lauren said, "I've had enough of this—this stalemate. What time do we leave in the morning?"

"Be ready by ten," he said curtly.

"Fine. I'll see you then." She put her glass down beside the sculpture and turned to leave.

"Stalemate or no, we're not finished with each other."

She looked back over her shoulder. He was standing very still, the lamp beside the leather couch throwing planes of light and shadow over his strongly carved features; the force of his willpower struck her like a blow. She said, "Until you make it clear you believe me—that I've never been promiscuous, that I haven't slept with anyone in four years—I'm keeping my distance. If we add Wallace to that equation, what have we got? Two people who shouldn't be sharing a drink, let alone a bed." She pushed a strand of hair back from her face. "Don't you see? Truth is what I strive for in my work. So this is desperately important to me…and if I sound preachy and self-righteous, I'm sorry."

He was gazing at her in a silence that screamed along her nerves and which she had to end. "Although please don't assume if you do believe me that I'll fall into your arms like a damson from a tree. I just plain don't want to get involved with you."

"Now you really are lying."

The more quietly he spoke, the more he scared her. "We struck a bargain," she said, "and we're damn well going to stick to it."

"You don't back down, do you?"

"You'd prefer me to grovel?"

He suddenly laughed outright, his teeth very white against his tanned skin. "I have difficulty imagining it."

"If I can act like I'm in love with you, a little groveling shouldn't be a problem," she said irritably. "Ten o'clock. I'll be ready."

"Lauren, it's not all acting. With either one of us."

She wasn't going to touch that one. "Good night," she said coldly, and swept out of the room as best she could when wearing tights and granny boots. As she got undressed in the bathroom, all her movements jerky and uncoordinated, her thoughts went 'round and 'round like hamsters on a wheel. I can't stand him. I want him. I can't wait until I see the last of him. How will it feel to say goodbye to him? I will not go to bed with him. But I want to. I want to.

She tossed her underwear on the nearest chair and reached for her nightgown; and as she did so, caught sight of herself in the long mirror on the wall. Slowly she straightened. Sculpture of an enraged woman, she thought dryly. Or, to be more accurate, of a frustrated woman. Didn't she, in her heart of hearts, crave for Reece to be here now, beside her, his gaze drinking in her creamy limbs and full breasts? His hands around her waist, pulling her back against his body? So that, once and for all, she could lay Sandor to rest? Or did Sandor have absolutely nothing to do with all this?

Her pulses racing, Lauren yanked on her nightgown and scrubbed her teeth with vicious energy. Then she jumped into bed and pulled the covers over her head.

She wasn't going to think about Reece. In bed or out. Only five more days.

CHAPTER SEVEN

To say that Lauren was awestruck by Reece's house in Whistler was an understatement. With Reece piloting his own helicopter, they'd flown up Howe Sound past a long range of snowcapped mountains, following the winding highway to the resort with its chalets and elegant ski lodges at the base of Blackcomb and Whistler mountains. The golf course was a swath of vivid green amid the tall evergreens; tourists were strolling along the walkways around the village shops.

The helicopter swung toward the lower slopes, then gently dipped down to land behind a house built of richly stained cedar and slabs of stone. The rotors stilled. They climbed out, and in the ringing silence, Reece said in a matter-of-fact voice, "Maureen and Graham look after the place. I have meetings all afternoon, and I've arranged a tour of the village for the wives. So you're free until seven-thirty. And tonight, please wear something that keeps you decently covered."

"What a concept," Lauren said.

His lips narrowed. "Tomorrow I'll be working in my office here, I've got some catching up to do. We'll leave for Vancouver Island the next morning."

The air smelled sweetly of pine and moss, and she had always loved being near mountains. Besides, she'd told Charlie she wouldn't lose her temper so often. Lauren said sincerely, "This is a beautiful place, Reece. I'm glad I'm here."

He looked her up and down, from her bulky wool

sweater to her slim-fitting jeans and polished loafers. "The sun's caught in your hair," he said huskily, "it's like a mixture of copper and bronze."

"There's no audience...you don't have to say things like that."

"I said it because I wanted to. Because it's true."

She flashed, "Do you believe it's true that there's been no one for me since Sandor?"

He hesitated. "I'm starting to, yes."

"Until you stop hedging your bets, you can keep your compliments."

"You're utterly different from anyone else I've ever met," Reece said with sudden explosive force. "I move with the jet set, where women trade lovers faster than stocks at the New York exchange. Where fidelity's considered old-fashioned and affairs are part of the entertainment."

She was seared by a jealousy all the more horrible for being so unexpected. "And where do you fit in that picture?"

Something changed in his face. "For the last few years, I haven't. I got tired of all the games. But I'd learned my lesson—wave your fortune in front of a woman and she's after you. Spend money on her and she's yours."

"Let me tell you the first lesson I learned in art school, Reece Callahan. Money can't buy talent—it's a gift. So your money's of absolutely no use to me."

"I've been getting that message all along." Again Reece hesitated, looking uncharacteristically unsure of himself. "If we leave Sandor out of the equation, there's still Wallace. Wallace did commit fraud, Lauren. The evidence is indisputable. I don't want you thinking I made it all up out of thin air."

She took a step backward. "He couldn't have! I just can't believe that of him."

"So you don't believe me—and I'm not ready to believe you."

The sun glittered on the needles of the pines, a bird squawked in the undergrowth, and through the trees she could see the mountain's stark outline, black and white against a blue sky. "I'm tired of fighting with you all the time," she said unhappily, "because it doesn't get us anywhere. Can't we just fulfill our bargain and leave it at that?"

"I don't know—can we?"

"Of course we can," she said shortly. "I'll see you at seven-thirty and I'll be a model of decorum."

"Decorum," he repeated ironically. "Well, that'll be a change."

"Hey, I've been adoring, brash and charming. Decorum's no sweat."

"The ABCs of our agreement? What about assertive, beautiful and confident?" He grinned at her, his teeth as white as the snow on the mountains. "Not that we should omit delectable, erotic and fiery."

"Or aggravating, bossy and controlling. Referring to you, of course."

He laughed. "And then there's deprived and extraordinarily frustrated."

"Tell me about it," she grimaced.

Reece shoved his hands in his pockets. "You know what?" he said. "I like you."

The breeze was playing with his hair; his smile was far too infectious. Hardening her heart, Lauren said, "You can't like someone who's a promiscuous liar."

"So I'm supposed to believe I'm the first man in four

years to turn you on?'' he retorted. ''When most of the time you hate my guts?''

Put like that, it did sound unbelievable. Lauren said crossly, ''Look at yourself in the mirror sometime. You're gorgeous. You've got a great body, and you breathe power and confidence. I'd have to be a chunk of marble not to respond to you.''

He said with matching irritation, ''Why do I feel like I've just been compared to a centerfold? Mr. Hunk-of-the-Month, guaranteed to turn you on, and all for five ninety-five.''

''It's your personality I have the problem with,'' she cried. ''Wallace couldn't have stolen from you, I'll never accept that—so how can I go to bed with someone who believes that the only man who ever treated me with anything like kindness was a common thief?''

''Maybe he was both,'' Reece said heavily. ''Kind to you and deceitful to me.''

''We're going around in circles,'' she said helplessly. ''And I'm sure you have more important things to do than stand here arguing with me.''

''I do. You're right. Seven-thirty sharp, Lauren.'' Then Reece turned on his heel and vanished through the trees, leaving Lauren with a sweet-scented breeze and an oddly hollow heart.

If she'd been completely truthful with Reece, she'd have put a stranglehold around his neck and kissed him sense-less. And how was that for inconsistency?

Prompt at seven-thirty Reece discovered Lauren in the huge living room, with its vista of mountains and sky, augmented by an expanse of glass, a granite fireplace and a massive Haida carving of a killer whale. Lauren, not to his surprise, was standing in front of the whale, her head to one side. He said, suppressing a surge of pleasure that she should be here in a house that he loved, "A young carver from the Queen Charlotte Islands did that. What do you think?"

"It's wonderful," she said softly. "So obviously symbolic, yet so fully alive."

It was exactly what he'd thought when he'd first seen it. Disliking an intimacy of thought that could, perhaps, be as strong a tie as any bodily intimacy, he ordered, "Let me look at you."

She turned around, her eyes demurely downcast. Her black satin pants were topped with a tangerine embroidered jacket, high-collared and long-sleeved. Her hair was smoothed into a long plait down her back, and her makeup minimal. He said, trying to subdue the laughter that wanted to escape his chest, "How did you get rid of your curls?"

"Gloop," she said.

With a touch of grimness, he added, "You have a persona for every occasion."

"That's the deal."

"I rue the day you walked into my office—I haven't had a moment's peace since."

"I hear the doorbell," she responded, and laid her hand lightly on his sleeve. "Shall we greet our guests, dear?"

He was almost taken in, so soft was the curve of her lips, so sweet her smile. Keep your head, Reece, and don't give her the satisfaction of knowing you want to undo every single button on that embroidered thing she's wearing and caress her breasts until she begs on bended knee to be in your bed.

After that, the evening seemed to go on forever, weighted by a formality that normally Reece enjoyed. The food was delicious, from sushi to tempura; from his position cross-legged on the floor, he watched Lauren charm the guests in her vicinity. She was being a perfect hostess. His mother would have approved of her, and suggested in her well-bred voice that he marry her; Clea, his sister, would have adored her. And Lauren, unless he was very much mistaken, would have liked Clea. More than she liked him, for sure.

Clea, younger than he by seven years, dead these five years...

As always, his thoughts slammed to a stop. After all this time, he still couldn't bring himself to remember the last day they'd spent together, the casualness with which he'd left her on the sidewalk outside the bank in Chicago, without the slightest premonition that he would never see her alive again. His fingers tightened around the stem of his glass. Stop it, he thought savagely. There's no point in thinking about it. It's over. Over and done with.

Then he suddenly found himself looking up, aware almost instinctually of being watched. Lauren's turquoise eyes jolted into his; she was gazing straight at him, such compassion on her face that for a moment he longed simply to take her in his arms, put his cheek to her hair and pour out to her everything that had happened that fateful afternoon. An afternoon that had marked him forever.

Oh, sure, he thought caustically, what would you do that for? You've never told anyone how you feel about Clea's death, so why would you start with Lauren Courtney? With a deliberation he knew would wound her, he hardened his features against her, shutting her out as effectively as if he'd turned his back on her; and watched her eyes darken with pain. Then her gaze dropped to her plate. Her neighbor on her right asked her a question. She fumbled for an answer, her cheeks as pale as the delicate porcelain plates they were eating from.

Clea wouldn't have approved of the way he'd behaved. But Clea was dead.

Clea was the reason he'd bought the statue of the Madonna and child; somehow it symbolized all that she'd lost.

Longing to be alone, Reece smiled at the elderly gentleman across from him, and asked about a temple he'd visited on one of the northern islands; minute by minute the time went by, until eventually he and Lauren were standing in the wide front door saying the last of their goodbyes. He raised his hand in a salute as the final car vanished down the driveway and closed the door on the cool, pine-scented darkness. "That went very well," he said.

Lauren didn't even bother to respond. Resting her hand on his sleeve, she asked with the directness he'd come to expect from her, "What were you thinking about at the dinner table, Reece? You looked devastated."

His earlier brief impulse to confide in her had buried itself under the layers of reserve that had been his only defense all those years ago. He said bitingly, "The lousy stock market index? The fact I'm going to have to fire my Thailand CEO? You're the one who keeps insisting we stick to our bargain, so why don't you keep your curiosity to yourself?"

"Can't you admit you're human like the rest of us?" she implored. "Do you think the world would come to an end if you said that sometimes you hurt?"

"Shut up," Reece grated.

Her fingers tightened on his sleeve. Biting her lip, she said, "I saw your face...you looked haunted. Whatever happened, or whatever you did—it couldn't be so bad that you can't tell me about it."

He stared down at her hand as though he'd never seen

it before. No rings. Tangerine polish on her nails. Unhealed cuts on two of her fingers. These were the fingers that had carved the statue in her bedroom, so pervaded with ageless emotion that his throat had closed when he'd seen it. These same fingers two nights ago had stroked his belly and lain against his rib cage, warm and strong, filling him with a primitive desire more intense than any he'd ever known.

She wanted his body, yes. But she wanted his soul, too. And that she couldn't have. It wasn't up for grabs.

He picked up her hand, lifted it from his sleeve and let it drop. Then he said coldly, "Your imagination's functioning overtime and your pushiness turns me off. Go to bed, Lauren."

Her lashes flickered under the dark wings of her brows. Then, with a courage he had to admire, she raised her chin. Her voice perfectly level, she said, "You may have lots of money, Reece. But you're poor in the things that matter. Like intimacy. And sharing."

"Keep your pop psychology—I don't need it."

"You don't need anything. Or anyone. Least of all me," she said very quietly. Then she turned on her heel and walked away from him.

Her hips swayed in her satin trousers; her back was very straight. He fought down the crazy urge to call her back, to hold her to his heart and describe that sunny afternoon in Chicago, the blood on the sidewalk, the crowds, the police and the sirens. The guilt that had seized him by the throat and never let him go.

No, he thought. No way. You're a loner, Reece Callahan. And you'd damn well better stay that way. Just because a woman with eyes like a tropical sea and hair like burnished teak thinks you should bare your soul is no reason to do so.

She'd disappeared down the hallway that led to her bedroom. But she'd disappeared from more than his sight, he knew that in his bones. Lauren Courtney was a proud woman. She wouldn't beg him for anything.

She'd stick to the terms of their bargain because she was also an honorable woman; but on Saturday night she'd vanish from his life just as she'd vanished to her room.

Game over.

Cursing under his breath, Reece headed for his own bedroom; and seven hours later got up after a sleep broken by nightmares in which Clea and Lauren were screaming for help and he was unable to reach either one of them. Feeling as though he'd been beaten over the head with a baseball bat, he staggered to the shower. Half an hour later, clean-shaven, dressed in a navy-blue suit and looking, he hoped, minimally better, he strode into the breakfast room. But Lauren wasn't alone. There were two people in the room.

Sam Lewis, his protégé and at one time Clea's boyfriend, was standing at the window looking out. Lauren was at his side, laughing at something Sam had just said; they looked at ease with each other, young and carefree. Reece said sharply, "Sam—what are you doing here?"

Sam turned, a grin still on his narrow, pleasant face which was topped with black curls. "Hi, there, Reece. I was in Vancouver on business, and found out from Maureen that you were here. So I came up to say hello."

Lauren had also turned. She was wearing tailored cargo pants with a crisp white shirt, her braided hair gleaming in the sun. She said coolly, "Good morning, Reece. Sam and I were just discussing hiking in the mountains for the day."

Subduing an emotion he refused to label jealousy, Reece said, "Check the grizzly sightings before you go. And take bear spray, Sam." He sounded like an elderly uncle, he thought irritably, and with a sudden fierce intensity knew he was the one who should be going hiking with Lauren. Not Sam.

He couldn't go hiking with Lauren. For one thing he had to work all day. For another Lauren wouldn't go with him. Not after last night. Scowling, he poured himself a cup of coffee and stirred in more cream than was good for him. Sam said easily, "I'll check with the warden station before we leave. We'll probably take one of the lifts and hike in the alpine meadows—the view's incredible up there."

"Fine," Reece said briefly. They all sat down at the breakfast table, where Reece ate melon and strawberries that tasted like sawdust and listened as Sam described Whistler's ski slopes. Lauren looked heartbreakingly beautiful, he thought. With her hair swept back, the purity of her cheekbones and the arch of her brows had the elegant restraint of a medieval portrait.

She hadn't once met his gaze since he'd sat down. He said flatly, "Lauren, there's been a change of plan. I'd like you to go with the wives of the Japanese delegation to Pemberton tomorrow morning—they'll be having brunch at the golf club there. The bus will get back here about three and we'll leave at five in the 'copter."

She raised her brows. "Whatever you say. I should explain, Sam, that I've been acting as a hostess for Reece the last few days—I'm heading back to Manhattan early next week."

"I see," said Sam in the kind of voice that meant he didn't see at all but was too polite to ask for details.

"If I'm on duty tomorrow," Lauren went on, "I'd better enjoy my day off today," and gave Sam the full benefit of her generous smile.

Sam, Reece noticed with a flare of pure rage, looked dazzled. "Maybe I could have a word with you after breakfast, Sam," he said in a tone of voice that was an order, not a request. "How long are you staying?"

"Tomorrow morning, if that's okay. I'm flying back to Boston midafternoon to work on the Altech proposal. Which I presume is what you want to talk to me about."

It wasn't. Ten minutes later, when Reece had ushered Sam into his office and closed the door, he said abruptly, "I want to make something clear. Under no circumstances are you to tell Lauren about Clea."

Sam stood a little taller, a new maturity in his thin face. "Clea and I were in love," he said, "she was one of the most important people in my life. And she's been dead for five years. Why can't I tell Lauren about her if I want to?"

"Lauren and I have a business arrangement," Reece said. "Clea's death has nothing to do with her."

"Maybe you should tell her about Clea yourself," Sam said stringently.

Reece held on hard to his temper. "There's no need. You heard what she said—she's going back to Manhattan very soon. And my private life is precisely that—private. So please don't mention Clea's name."

"All right," Sam said. "Although I think you're wrong."

"You've changed in the last while," Reece said slowly.

"Yeah...finally growing up." Sam grinned. "These negotiations you've been having me do...it's a sink or swim process. So I've been studying some Olympic-class types, watching how they manage. You among them."

Reluctantly Reece smiled; he'd always liked Sam, and with an inner wince of pain remembered how happy he'd been all those years ago with Clea's choice of partner. Quickly he shifted the conversation to business matters, and twenty minutes later watched through his study window as Sam and Lauren climbed into Sam's rented car to drive to the ski lift on Blackcomb. What if Lauren fell in love with Sam? How would he feel about that?

Lauren in love with Sam—what difference would it make? He himself had no intention of ever falling in love, certainly not with a woman as contrary and elusive as Lauren Courtney.

Get to work, Reece. You know where you are in the world of business. You're in control in that world.

So what did that imply? That he was out of control where Lauren was concerned? That he was running away from something?

Swearing under his breath, Reece turned on his computer and took some papers out of his briefcase.

CHAPTER EIGHT

LAUREN enjoyed Sam's brief visit. After Reece's inexplicable mood changes, Sam's straightforward pleasure in her company was a relief. Besides, he had the tact not to ask any questions about herself and Reece, questions she would have found difficult to answer. All the more difficult because as she hiked the high alpine meadows that day, part of her was wishing it was Reece who was with her. Reece, rather than Sam.

Who in the world would choose Reece's arrogance and emotional coldness over Sam's sunny nature? No woman in her right mind.

But when Sam took her hand to help her up a ridge, or when he brushed a mosquito from her arm, she felt absolutely nothing. Not the slightest twinge of desire. It had been the same with all the men she'd dated in the months since Sandor. In no way could she compare this with the fire in her blood whenever Reece touched her.

It'd be safe to go to the yacht club with Sam, she thought as she followed him to his car the next morning to say goodbye. Safe, sensible and prudent. Like her life the last four years.

Hugging Sam, she lifted her face as he kissed her on both cheeks. "It was lovely to meet you," she said sincerely. "Get in touch the next time you're in New York, won't you?"

"I will—I spend a fair bit of time there. Be sure you go kayaking while you're at the yacht club. 'Bye, Lauren."

Smiling, she waved as he drove away, then turned back

to the house. Three more days were left in the bargain she'd struck with Reece. Then she could head home. Back to her normal life, with its hard work, its routines and pleasures. Back where she belonged.

Didn't she?

She opened the door and stepped inside. Reece was standing so close she could have reached out and touched him. He snarled, "On Saturday do you plan to embrace me with the same enthusiasm?"

She said incredulously, "You're jealous!"

"Don't make me laugh."

"I don't plan to hug you at all."

"Did you keep to the terms of our bargain, Lauren? Or did you tell him all about Wallace and what a son of a bitch I am?"

"Difficult though it may be for you to believe, we didn't talk about you at all."

"So did you kiss him—up there in the mountains when the two of you were alone together?"

Her shoulders sagged, anger deserting her to be replaced by a despair that frightened her with its intensity. "You still think I'm up for grabs by the first man that comes along, don't you, Reece? You'd rather believe Sandor, a man you've never met, than the woman who's standing right in front of you... You don't know how I'm longing for the weekend—it can't come too soon."

"That's entirely mutual," he grated. "The bus will pick you up here in an hour. Be ready at five to leave for the island." Then he strode away from her down the hall.

Lauren watched him go. The only thing Reece could give her was orders, she thought painfully. It didn't seem like much.

* * *

The last of the tankers traveling through the wide strait between the mainland and Vancouver Island fell behind as the helicopter swept toward a cluster of small islands set like unpolished emeralds in a turquoise sea. A yacht in full sail looked the size of a child's toy; a group of kayaks floated like matchsticks on the tide. Then Reece began the descent, and through the rounded window Lauren sighted the peaks of the yacht club roof nestled in the trees.

She couldn't imagine a more exquisite location. If only she were here alone, free to roam to her heart's content. Making no attempt to hide the defiance in her tone, she spoke into the headset. "Tomorrow morning I'm going kayaking."

"Not alone, you're not."

"Then I'll just have to find someone to go with me, won't I? With my reputation, that shouldn't be difficult."

"Lay off, Lauren. Unless you want me to land in the woods."

She bit her lip, unwillingly admiring the interplay of feet and hands as Reece brought the helicopter to the very center of the landing pad. When the rotors had stilled, an attendant came for their luggage and the manager ushered them to the east wing of a building that fitted the landscape seamlessly. He opened a door at the very end of the wing. "The bedroom's through there, the bathroom's to your right, and the living room's set up with a bar and all the amenities. Your client will meet you at the main bar at seven, Mr. Callahan, and dinner's at eight."

Lauren scarcely heard the last part of his speech. Bedroom. Wasn't that what he'd said? Bedroom. In the singular. As he left the room, she marched across the living area, yanked open the two doors and discovered that the first led into a palatial bathroom and the second into a bedroom, furnished with a vast king-size bed. Bedroom and bed, both in the singular. She said furiously, "This isn't in the bargain, Reece—that we share a bed. How *dare* you do this to me?"

He said impatiently, "I made the arrangements weeks ago, before I knew you existed. Anyway, that bed's big enough that we never need come within three feet of each other."

"I will not sleep with you!"

"Then you can sleep on the sofa."

He'd gone too far. On top of last week, it was one thing too many. Her fury evaporated and to her utter consternation Lauren, who never cried, burst into tears, noisy and copious tears that wouldn't stop no matter how hard she tried. Burying her face in her hands, she stumbled toward the bathroom, desperate for privacy. Then Reece took her by the shoulders, guiding her toward the bed. Striking out at him, she sobbed, "Leave me alone—I can't bear you to touch me. Oh, God, why did I ever *do* this?"

Reece thrust her down on the bed, put his arm around her and said in a voice she hadn't heard him use before, "Don't cry, Lauren. Please don't cry."

"I'll cry if I want to," she wept, her breath hiccuping in her throat. "I just can't take this anymore."

He pulled her to his chest so that her sobs were muffled against his shirt, his hands rubbing her back and her shoulders, his cheek resting on her hair in a way that, at some far remove, felt altogether perfect; and perhaps it was this that finally brought Lauren's breathing under control. "I never cry," she snuffled, "never. Not even Sandor made me cry, or all those horrible newspaper articles. What's *wrong* with me?"

"Why don't you ever cry, Lauren?"

The tears seemed to have unlocked her tongue. "I learned not to. Years ago when Wallace left, my mother wouldn't allow me to cry for him. And then the older I got, and the more obviously attractive, the more she resented me and wanted me out of the house. Which hurt. A lot. But I was too proud to cry in front of her and somehow I guess I lost the knack.''

''Do you ever see your mother?''

''Oh, sometimes. We're excruciatingly polite, just as though nothing's wrong, and it's so false I hate it. My second stepfather's very conservative and very dull—just for the record, he believes Sandor, too. Which doesn't exactly make me warm to him.''

''Any more than you've warmed to me.''

''Do you blame me?'' she said with a spark of her normal spirit.

''So let me get this straight…you're sleeping on the sofa tonight,'' Reece went on in an odd voice.

''You're darn right I am. Since you're not being chivalrous and offering me the bed.''

''I'm not the one with the problem,'' Reece said. ''Why won't you share the bed with me?''

She rolled her eyes. ''Do I have to spell it out? You know what happened when I kissed you that time—and you think I'm going to sleep within fifteen feet of you? Give me a break.''

''So you want me.''

''I've been celibate for four years and you're not normally this dull-witted.''

''You want me, yet you're going to spend the night on a sofa that was chosen more for elegance than comfort because you won't risk us making love. That doesn't spell promiscuity to me.''

''Wow,'' she said. ''Imagine that.''

With sudden intensity he took her by the shoulders. ''I want to trust you, don't you see? By God, I want to.''

"Then do it," she said in exasperation.

"Yeah...just like that." He hesitated. "Do you really hate my guts?"

"How would I know?"

"There's no one else to ask," Reece said dryly.

"I need to blow my nose," she announced, then tugged free of him and marched to the bathroom. In the gold-edged mirrors she scowled at her reflection, transferring the scowl to Reece as he came to stand beside her. "I look a fright."

"You do."

A reluctant smile tipped her mouth. "If I'm to resemble even remotely the seductive hostess of a very rich man, I've got some serious work to do on my face. Out, Reece."

His eyes were smiling into hers in the mirror; his height, the breadth of his shoulders, the strong line of his jaw all entranced her, with an attraction so strong that Lauren was suddenly frightened out of her wits. What would happen if she gave in to it? Wouldn't she regret it for the rest of her life? She forced herself to look away, leaning into the mirror to wipe a tearstain from her cheek. "Cocktails in twenty minutes," she said. "We'd better hurry."

"Do you plan to keep in touch with Sam?"

Her head snapped up. "Yes."

"But not with me."

"No."

The jaw she'd been admiring tightened ominously. "So what's the difference?"

"Sam's a goldfish, you're a shark."

"You sure know how to make a man feel good," Reece rasped. Swinging her around to face him, he planted a very angry kiss full on her mouth, then let her go so abruptly that she had to clutch the edge of the polished granite counter for support.

Her fingers gripping the cold stone, she erupted, "You seem to think you can kiss me any time you feel like it, then push me away as if I was nothing but a chunk of wood."

"You look even more beautiful when you're angry," he said with as much emotion as if he really were discussing a chunk of wood. "I'll go and arrange for a kayak for you tomorrow morning—you're to be back in time for lunch."

"I can arrange my own kayak!"

"And you'll go with a guide—that's an order."

Another order. As he strode out of the bathroom, Lauren pulled a hideous face in the mirror. She then got dressed in an orange silk pantsuit and slathered on makeup to hide the marks of her crying jag. So Reece was beginning to trust her. This should have made her happy; and instead only deepened her fear. Why could she take risks with bronze and wood and not with a living, red-blooded man?

If she had the answer to that question, she'd probably be sharing the king-size bed with Reece.

Lauren didn't share the bed with Reece. After an evening during which she smiled until her jaw ached, she spent a night twisting and turning on the sofa, by four a.m. convinced it had been upholstered by a sadist. It was a relief to get up at six-thirty and head for the dining room for an early breakfast before she went kayaking; but ten minutes later, Reece joined her at her table.

"I decided to go with you," he said.

She'd been longing for a few hours away from him; as the end of their bargain came nearer, her whole nervous system was winding itself tighter and tighter. Her dismay must have shown in her face. Reece said tersely, "Hating my guts is beginning to seem like a very mild term for the way you feel about me."

"I was brought up to be polite."

"Then smile at me, darling," he said in a silky under-tone, "the waitress is coming." Lifting her hand to his lips, he nibbled at her fingertips.

As heat coursed through Lauren's veins, she swayed toward him. The waitress said formally, "Have you had the chance to look at the menu, madam?"

A blush stained Lauren's cheeks. "Fruit salad, toast and coffee, please," she babbled. Surely those were common enough items to be on any menu?

"And you, sir?"

Reece ordered, the waitress left and Reece said in a harsh whisper, "Every other woman I've ever had any-thing to do with has been an open book to me. But not you. You say you hate me and then you gaze at me as though you'd like to eat me for breakfast."

That was exactly the way she'd felt. For a wild moment Lauren was tempted to tell him they should skip the kay-aking, go back to the bedroom and truly share the king-size bed. But what if Reece were then to give her the same message as Sandor: that she was a failure in bed, awkward and unresponsive, her beauty useless to her and to anyone else? She couldn't bear that. It had been too humiliating, too shameful.

She was afraid to go to bed with Reece. She'd rather face New York's toughest art critics than the blue-eyed man sitting across from her at the table.

"Lauren, what's wrong? You look so unhappy."

The concern in his voice almost undid her. "Nothing that tomorrow won't fix," she mumbled, digging the tines of her fork into the linen cloth.

He said tautly, "Let's strike a deal. Let's forget about Wallace and our bargain and that goddamned king-size bed and go out kayaking. Sunshine, tides and the sound of water...and maybe some killer whales. How about it?"

The fork blurred in her vision; she was on the verge of crying again. Oh, God, what was the matter with her? "Sounds like a plan," she faltered.

"Good. I'm familiar with the area where they've been sighting the whales, so we'll head straight there...the salmon migrations were late this year, that's why they're still around."

Lauren managed something like a smile. "Instead of a shark, I should have compared you to a killer whale."

"Not likely—they live in family groups," he said, then added abruptly, "Good, here comes the coffee. Only way to start the day, wouldn't you agree?"

He hadn't meant to say anything about families, Lauren thought, stirring cream into her coffee and gazing at her attractively arranged plate of fruit. As the waitress moved away, she said, "I've never asked you about your family."

"Nothing to tell...my parents are dead."

"No brothers or sisters?"

After a fractional pause, he said, "No."

He was lying; she was almost certain of it. She speared a ripe strawberry with her fork, saying, "I was an only child. Every Christmas from age five to eight I wrote an impassioned letter to Santa Claus asking for a little sister to be left under the tree. Then one of my friends told me Santa didn't exist." Her smile was rueful. "The pains of growing up. Did you ever want a brother or sister?"

"I had a sister. She died."

There was a small, dreadful silence. Lauren put her fork down. "Reece, I'm so sorry."

"It was a long time ago. Closed book. You should take sunscreen this morning—the light reflecting off the water can give you a bad burn."

The skin was taut over Reece's knuckles; his eyes were hooded. He hadn't meant to tell her about his sister, that was obvious. However she'd died, and however long ago, the pain of her death was still very much alive.

Lauren longed to comfort him. Yet tomorrow afternoon when they arrived back in Vancouver, she was planning to turn her back on him. *No,* she'd said, *I won't keep in touch with you.*

Did she mean that? Could she simply turn her back on a man who made her angrier than she'd ever been in her life, whose body entranced her, whose character baffled and fascinated her in equal measure? What if she never saw him again? Was that what she wanted?

She took a mouthful of raspberries and ate them as though they were made of Styrofoam. When in the last four years had she felt as alive, as vital as she had in Reece's company? As frustrated, as happy and as furious? After Sandor, she'd buried herself in her work and neglected her sexuality, her very ordinary needs for intimacy. Her career had benefited. But what about the rest of her?

"Did you hear what I said?" Reece demanded.

"S-sorry?"

"I asked how much kayaking experience you'd had."

She struggled to gather her thoughts. "Oh, quite a lot. With friends in Maine."

"Will you give me your home phone number?"

She blinked. "I—yes. If you'll do the same."

"I have a number where I can always be reached, I'll give you that."

"Why, Reece?" she said faintly.

"God knows," he said in a raw voice. "I just can't stand to say goodbye tomorrow and never see you again."

"I feel the same way." She produced the ghost of a smile. "But—like you—don't ask me to explain."

He said flatly, "I don't believe Sandor anymore. I'm sorry I ever did."

A sliver of melon fell back on her plate. Feeling as though the earth had shifted beneath her feet, she whispered, "If I start to cry again, then you won't believe me that I never cry."

"You've never used your sexuality to further your career, have you?"

"Not unless you count Sandor in that category."

"I don't. You were young. You were no doubt starry-eyed about being in Manhattan. And he was your mentor."

"I was in love with him. At least, I thought I was. Until one day he stole a design of mine and then denied it—and that was the end of that."

With sudden vigor Reece said, "Let's go kayaking, Lauren. Now. I've had enough of the past and the fact that you and I lose our tempers with each other five times a day."

"Ten times."

"I refuse to argue about it," he laughed, pushing back his chair. "How's that for restraint?"

It was she who was exercising restraint, Lauren thought. When he laughed like that he looked so carefree, so vital, so overwhelmingly male that it was as much as she could do to keep her hands off him.

He believed her about Sandor. And he wanted her phone number. A big grin on her face, she followed him out of the dining room.

CHAPTER NINE

THE waters of the strait were jade-green, thick strands of bull kelp aligned with the tide that surged between the islands. An eagle watched from a tall hemlock as the two kayaks passed; a seal slipped from the granite into the water. An hour after they'd set out, Reece said in a low voice, "Whales have been seen in this area. The tide's just right, let's hang around for a while."

"It's so beautiful," Lauren sighed.

For once Reece was blind to the scenery; he had eyes only for Lauren. His mouth dry, he watched the sun on her profile as she drank in the graceful sweep of cedars and the dazzling white gulls that soared so effortlessly through the channels. She was totally unlike any other woman he'd ever wanted; he'd been a fool to judge her by stereotypes and secondhand reports.

He had to bed her. Soon.

Before they went their separate ways tomorrow? Was that what he wanted? To put some sort of claim on her, to say in the most primitive way possible to her and to the rest of the world that she was his? And his alone?

She'd been happy that he'd asked for her phone number.

"Reece," Lauren said in an urgent whisper, "what's that?"

A dark snout had lifted itself from the water. Then the body followed in a sleek curve, the stark pattern of black and white dramatic and unmistakable. In a swoosh the whale blew, the mist hanging in the air as the tail vanished beneath the sea, leaving only ripples on the water. Then

99

three more whales surfaced, one much smaller than the other two. Their bodies arched with infinite grace, then they too were gone. The water rocked and was still.

The first whale reemerged, twisting higher in the air, its flippers gleaming in the sun; it slapped down on the water, spray flying in all directions. A few moments later, the waves lifted the hull of Reece's kayak. He spared a glance for Lauren. Her face was entranced. Would she look like that when he made love to her?

How long was he willing to wait?

The whales reappeared twice more. Then the water became once again an unbroken swath of dark green silk. Lauren said softly, "That was wonderful...thanks so much for bringing me here, Reece."

"A pleasure," he said with a crooked grin. "Want to see some Kwakiutl rock carvings?"

She smiled back, an uncomplicated smile of pure delight. "What do you think?"

"Oh, I'm censoring my thoughts," he said lightly.

"Maybe it's just as well we're in separate kayaks."

"You could try sharing the bed tonight."

"On the strength of exchanging our phone numbers? I don't think so."

She sounded very adamant. Too adamant? He said casually, "We'll paddle between those two islands, the carvings are only ten minutes away."

She shot him a fulminating look. "Why do you want to make love to me, Reece? So tomorrow you can kiss me goodbye and go on to your next woman?"

"I've never operated that way!"

"You've never been in love, either. Never let a woman close to you. Are you going to tell me how your sister died?"

Bloodstains on a city sidewalk... His paddle hit the water at the wrong angle and his boat slewed sideways. "No."

"You're only interested in one kind of intimacy, that's your problem."

"We're arguing again, Lauren."

"The alternative seems to be for me to do exactly as you please."

Throwing her weight into her stroke, she dug her paddle into the water. Reece said innocently, "Want some chocolate-coated almonds?"

"You drive me crazy," she exclaimed, braking with one of her blades. "Yes, I do."

He brought his kayak closer to hers, reached in the pocket on his lifejacket and took out the package of almonds. But as she reached out her hand, Reece took her by the wrist, pulled her even closer and kissed her with lingering pleasure full on the mouth. His boat tipped dangerously. Releasing her with something less than finesse, he said, "You taste better than chocolate."

"Nicest compliment I've had all day. Well, the only one, actually."

He started to laugh, tipping some almonds into her palm. "You're as graceful as a killer whale, how about that?"

"You're like a chunk of granite. Unmovable."

"You're as beautiful as a sea cucumber," Reece said solemnly.

Earlier he'd pointed out some of the slimy, olive-green sea cucumbers that were draped over the rocks, their bulbous bodies adorned with livid red spots. "Yuk," said Lauren. "I know what you're like—the tides. Deep and dangerous."

"Dangerous?"

"Oh, yes," Lauren said, "very dangerous. I want some more almonds, then I want to see the rock carvings."

If only he didn't like her so much. If only he weren't convinced his money meant less than nothing to her. If only she wasn't so heartstoppingly beautiful...if none of these were true, would he be able to turn his back on her tomorrow? And what if he did seduce her? Would that bind her to him even more tenaciously?

Permanence wasn't in his plans. The one thing he'd learned from Clea's death was that there was no permanence. He tipped more of the almonds into her hand and said easily, "There's some incredible driftwood along the shoreline near the yacht club. I'll show you on the way back."

Lauren loved the rock carvings; but the driftwood induced in her a silence that Reece already recognized as her creativity going into high gear. As she wandered among the huge tangled roots and twisted branches, which were polished by the sea and bleached by the sun, he realized something else. The driftwood was free. He couldn't buy it for her. And he'd be willing to bet that given a choice of a fifty-carat diamond and a stump rounded like an ancient turtle, she'd take the stump.

He wasn't falling in love with her. Of course he wasn't. Falling in love, like permanence, wasn't on his list.

Lauren wandered back to him, her face abstracted. "I'm so glad you showed this to me."

Add generosity to her list of virtues, he thought, and fought against the temptation to strip her naked and bed her on the pale sand, where hemlocks whispered in the breeze and the driftwood would be their only witness. "I'll tow your kayak back, if you want to stay for a while," he offered. "You can walk back to the club from here."

Her smile was blinding. "Would you? That'd be wonderful."

As he paddled away from the beach, Reece was willing

to bet she'd already forgotten all about him. He wasn't sure whether to be angry or amused that she could so cavalierly dismiss him: that she was happy to be abandoned on a deserted beach in the wilderness. New experiences were supposed to stretch your character, he thought wryly. His must be way out of shape after a week in Lauren's company.

Not that that was permanent, either.

Lauren stayed on the beach for almost two hours. In the end, she lugged a relatively small piece of driftwood back to the club, its branches curved like waves rising from the sea. She knew exactly what she was going to do with it. Walking to the deck that wrapped around Reece's suite, she shrugged off her lifejacket, went inside and got right to work. Reece didn't come back for lunch; at four in the afternoon, she realized she was extremely hungry. She'd have a quick shower and get something to eat from room service.

Bundling her hair under a plastic cap, Lauren let the water beat on her shoulders and arms. The work she'd done in the last few hours had been deeply satisfying; but she was honest enough to realize she was also using it as escapism. In twenty-four hours, she and Reece would go their separate ways, he to London, she back to Charlie's, and thence to her studio in Manhattan. Worlds apart.

She was dreading the moment when they'd actually say goodbye; dreading it with a poignancy that had her nervous system on red alert. As the water streamed down her breasts and thighs, she wondered with an inner shiver of desire what it would be like to have Reece's hands roam her body. If she made love with him, what barriers between them would fall? What would she learn about this man of contradictions, so complex and private, so forceful and intense? And what would she learn about herself? That she wasn't the failure Sandor had labeled her?

She mustn't even think this way. Because once Reece returned to his true milieu, he'd forget all about her and their ridiculous bargain.

She closed her eyes, letting the water lave her face. She'd called him dangerous. But her own thoughts were even more dangerous. Jerkily Lauren turned off the gold taps and stepped onto the mat, wrapping herself in a luxuriously soft towel. Pulling off her shower cap, she shook out her hair and walked out to the bedroom to get clean clothes. With her free hand, she picked out a long skirt of fine wool and an embroidered shirt, tossed them on the chair and rummaged in the drawer for underwear.

A man strode into the bedroom, flipping through a sheaf of papers. Reece.

As Lauren gave an exclamation of dismay, her hand slipped, the towel exposing the creamy slopes of her breasts. Reece stopped dead in his tracks. His papers dropped to the floor. He said hoarsely, "Oh, God, Lauren, you're exquisite..."

And then she was in his arms, and he was kissing her as though she was the only woman in the world and he the only man. As though she was his heart's desire, she thought dizzily, and felt the first imperious thrust of his tongue. The towel slipped further. As she made a frantic grab for it, he stayed her hand. "I want to see you," he said thickly. "All of you."

"But—"

He drew the folds of the towel away from her body, his eyes drinking in her full breasts, the sweet curves from waist to hip, the nest of dark hair at the juncture of her thighs. Then he dropped the towel to the floor to join his papers. With one hand he ripped at the buttons of his shirt, with the other traced the swell of her breast to its tip.

Fire streaked her flesh. She gasped with mingled shock and pleasure, in a wild surge of hope wondering if she might not, with Reece, enter a country she'd never traveled before. One from which Sandor had barred her. She swayed toward Reece as he tossed his shirt on the foot of the bed, her nipples rasped by his body hair, her flesh pierced again by that elusive streak of fire.

He took her face in his hands, kissing her with such passionate intensity that Lauren forgot all the reasons why she shouldn't be doing this. Forgot everything but the heat of his skin and her longing to be released from all her old fears and inadequacies. Dimly she sensed him fumbling with his belt; then he pushed her back on the bed, falling on top of her.

He was naked, fully aroused, his weight pinioning her. She made a tiny sound in her throat, for this was going too fast and beneath it all she realized she was still afraid. He muttered, "Dearest Lauren," and kissed her again, his tongue seeking hers, his hands roaming her body just as she'd fantasized in the shower. His palms clasped her waist, lifting her and arching her body to his, his mouth sliding down her throat to her breasts. As he took one rosy tip and teased it between his teeth, she gasped with delight.

"Reece, oh, please, yes…"

But before the fire could encompass her, he had moved from there like a man driven, assailing her with a host of sensations too sudden and too shattering to assimilate. She sought for words, and in a frightening flashback remembered how often with Sandor she'd tried to explain what she wanted, only to end up feeling that somehow she'd failed him.

She didn't want to fail Reece. But neither did she want

to fail herself. As Reece's fingers sought for and found the soft, wet cleft between her thighs, she said urgently, "Reece, I—"

"Yes," he muttered huskily, "you want me as much as I want you, don't you, my darling?" and thrust deep within her.

Again fear was eclipsed by wonderment. She clutched him by the shoulders, glorying in his strength and fierce impulsions, and cried out his name in a broken voice that she scarcely recognized as her own. As though it was all the signal he needed, his mouth plummeted to hers. As she opened to him, she brought his hand to her breast, aching for that streak of fire; but before it could reach her, she felt him break within her, a deep throbbing that both excluded her yet was so intensely intimate that she wanted to weep.

His heart was pounding against her ribs, his quickened breathing stirred her hair. He said thickly, "Lauren, beautiful Lauren...oh, God, that was much too fast, but I've desired you for so long. Too long. Let's spend the rest of the day in bed, so we can—" His eyes fell on his watch, still on his wrist. In utter consternation, he said, "I left the meeting to get those papers...they'll be wondering where I am." Sudden laughter gleamed in his eyes. "I don't think I'll tell them. What do you think?"

Through a haze of frustration and despair, Lauren managed to find her voice. "None of their business," she said raggedly. Yet her heart was tripping in her breast, for surely that was tenderness shining from his eyes and warming his smile. Tenderness and concern.

"Sweetheart," he said, "I've got to go, but I'll be back as soon as I can—give me two hours. Why don't you stay just where you are, and we'll pick this up where we left off? Because this is only the beginning, you know that, don't you?''

She didn't. But she produced a creditable smile of her own, saying almost too casually, ''I'll tidy your papers while you get dressed.''

But the first thing she did was find the towel and knot it firmly above her breasts, knowing she didn't want to be naked in front of him anymore. The papers were still in order; she aligned them carefully and passed them to him as he finished doing up his shirt, her eyes somewhere at the level of the top button. He said urgently, ''Lauren, I shouldn't have fallen on you like that, it all happened too quickly. But when I saw you, I—''

''You'd better hurry,'' she said with another of those meaningless smiles, smoothing his shirtfront so she wouldn't have to look at him.

''Yeah…'' He gave her a quick, fierce kiss. ''We've got the whole night,'' he said huskily. ''A whole night for me to show you how much I want you.''

He jammed his feet in his loafers and turned away. A moment later Lauren heard the outer door close behind him. She flung open the closet, grabbing a pair of bush pants and a shirt. She had to get out of here. Out of the bedroom. Out of the club. Go somewhere where she could think.

The beach, she thought. The beach with the driftwood. That's where she'd go. Maybe there she could make some sense out of a lovemaking that had tantalized her with what might have been, yet had withheld true fulfillment.

Hadn't it simply proved Sandor right? That she was a cold woman, whose creativity and imagination stopped short of the bed? Pain flooded her heart. Reece had had no problem unleashing his passion. So what was wrong with her?

Desperate to be outdoors, she went through the patio doors to the deck, going down the steps and crossing in front of the club. There was an attractive wild garden flanking the dining room; as she ducked beneath a dogwood tree, a voice said cheerily, "Hi, there, Lauren. What are you up to?"

She gave a nervous start. "Oh, Ray," she said. "I—I was just out for a walk."

She'd met Ray Hardy and his wife Diane last night at dinner, and had warmed to them both. They'd won a lottery four years ago, and now were taking a great deal of pleasure in spending their gains. Their enormous powerboat, *Winner,* was moored in the bay.

"Another nice day," Ray said contentedly. "We plan to leave shortly—Diane's got a hankering to do some shopping in Vancouver, and I've had enough of hanging around these financial types. Don't get me wrong, your Reece is a fine fella, just a touch too high-powered for me."

For me, too, Lauren thought unhappily. "You seemed to be holding your own at dinner last night."

"Decided when I won all that money I should learn a bit about looking after it. A couple of financiers took me for a ride before I smartened up—that's why I pay attention to a guy like Reece, you can see he's honest as the day's long."

It was an interesting perspective on Reece. Even though part of her was desperate to be alone, Lauren was reluctant to hurt Ray's feelings by hurrying off. "I'm sorry you got cheated out of some of your money."

"I said to the second one, 'Wallace,' I said, 'you're the real loser here because you get to live with yourself.' Not that that recovered any of my losses, mind you—but I felt a whole lot better for saying it."

Lauren's brain had stopped dead. Wallace meant one person to her—one person only. It couldn't be the same man. *"Wallace?"* she repeated faintly.

"That's right. Wallace Harvarson. Charming fella, all the right connections, but crooked as the branches on this tree."

Lauren clutched the trunk of the tree, her head whirling. "You're saying Wallace Harvarson cheated you out of a lot of money?" she said incredulously. "Are you sure?"

"Sure as I'm standing here... Hey, what's up? You don't look so good."

She said weakly, "Wallace was my stepfather. Wallace is the reason I'm with Reece."

Ray took her by the elbow and steered her toward a cedar bench tucked in the shade. "Now you sit right down and tell me what's the matter," he ordered. "I feel real bad that I've upset you like this."

His plump face was full of genuine concern. As briefly as she could, Lauren described the bargain between her and Reece. "I didn't believe a word Reece said—I couldn't imagine that Wallace, whom I adored, had been responsible for fraud. But he must have been. If he cheated you, he cheated Reece, too. Oh, God, I've been such a fool. Such a blind, stupid fool."

She pressed her palms to her cheeks. The evidence Reece had spoken of at their first meeting had been real, not fabricated; how he must have laughed at her impassioned defense of a man whose true character had been unknown to her. She'd been oblivious. She'd seen the man she'd wanted to see.

Ray said comfortingly, "Now then, you did what you thought best. This bargain to protect your stepfather's name—you did it in good faith, and that's what counts."

She said with true desperation, "I can't face Reece after this. I couldn't stand to see him again."

"Well, now, he did kind of take advantage of you."

In the most basic way possible, she thought miserably. Less than an hour ago in the big bed that overlooked the ocean. "Ray," she said urgently, "would you and Diane take me to Vancouver with you? Then I could get the first flight to New York—I really need to go home."

"Sure thing. Why don't you get your bags, and I'll bring the dinghy to meet you? That way they won't see you from the main desk... I kind of like to read spy stories," he explained apologetically.

"Give me five minutes," she said, and ran back to the wing where she and Reece were staying. It no longer mattered that she would be breaking the bargain. When Reece published the story of Wallace's fraud—because he would publish it, there'd be nothing stopping him—he'd be telling the truth. The stepfather she'd loved had been a figment of her imagination.

As pain engulfed her, she stumbled on the rough ground, throwing out a hand to keep her balance. A lovemaking that had confirmed all her fears, a revelation that had destroyed her beloved stepfather...how could she bear it?

She'd bear it because she had to. What she couldn't bear was to see Reece again. Because the worst thing of all was that she couldn't trust her own judgment. Wallace's many kindnesses had blinded her to his duplicity. Then she'd fallen under the spell of Sandor's charisma, only gradually realizing that his outward charm masked cruelty and a need to dominate.

What of Reece? What was he really like?

Drawing a long, jagged breath, she climbed up the slope to the deck and slipped through the door. Four minutes later she left by the same door, her suitcase in her hand, her driftwood sculpture in a plastic bag. She'd left the briefest of notes on the bed, its gist that she'd found out the truth about Wallace, that she was going home, and that she never wanted to see Reece again.

Ray had pushed the dinghy against the bank. She clambered in, positioning her case amidships and sitting where it would be hidden should anyone be watching from the club. They boarded *Winner* from the far side, and the crew started the engines. The wind blowing her hair around her face, Lauren watched the yacht club grow smaller, then vanish from sight as they rounded a pine-clad peninsula.

It wasn't Wallace she was thinking of. It was Reece. With every moment, as the wake spread behind them, she was being carried further and further from him; her whole body felt as if it, too, were being stretched, clinging to him in desperation.

She wasn't in love with him. She couldn't be: she'd told him she never wanted to see him again. So why did her heart feel as though it was being torn in two?

CHAPTER TEN

AT FIVE minutes after midnight, Lauren unlocked the door of her Manhattan studio. She was exhausted from jet lag and emotional stress; yet she was also wide awake, every nerve jangling. She put down her case and saw that the light on her telephone was flashing. Messages, waiting for her. Was there one from Reece?

Would he come after her?

A plan which had been playing in the back of her mind sprang fully-fledged into existence. She'd go to Maine. Now. She'd sell the house by the sea that Wallace had left her and she'd send the proceeds to Reece. She wouldn't get five hundred thousand for it, the full amount of Wallace's fraud; but she might get three. That would be a start.

It was the only way she knew to make reparation for the wrong Wallace had done.

Ignoring the telephone, she put on a pot of coffee in the kitchen, then found the key to the Maine property. Tossing the clothes she'd had at the yacht club on her bed, she quickly packed an overnight bag. She loved to drive. She'd take her time, stay at a couple of bed-and-breakfasts, try and sort out her life and get it back on track after an interlude that would surely, very soon, be relegated to the realm of temporary madness. The sooner forgotten, the better.

Once Lauren got out of the city, she drove steadily through the night; midmorning, she booked into a pleasant country inn, phoned Charlie to let her know where she was, then fell asleep like one stunned. When she woke up, she got in touch with a real estate agency in Maine that was near her house in Fox Cove. She then traveled along the coast the rest of the day. To her dismay, it was Reece who persisted in usurping her thoughts, rather than Wallace. Reece, whose hurried lovemaking had left her bereft.

She stayed the next night near the New Hampshire border, rather enjoying the sense of being in limbo, of no one knowing where she was. About noon the following day, she pulled up outside the house that Wallace had bequeathed her.

It was a restored saltbox house with white trim, set on an acre of prime property; in summer, roses and honeysuckle filled the air with their rich perfume, overlying the salt tang of the sea. Lauren had always planned to live in the house when she tired of New York. But how could she, now that she knew the property had come to her under false pretenses? From a man who'd been a liar and a cheat?

As she stood there, feeling the first deep ache of loss for a landscape she'd always loved, a silver Mercedes drew up behind her. The large voluble woman who climbed out was named Marjorie; she was the real estate agent and had already found a buyer. "He went 'round it yesterday, and he's submitted an offer, along with a postdated cheque," she said. "Rather irregular, but he's had his eye on it for months, so he was delighted to hear it was for sale and didn't want anyone else beating him to it. This can all be cleared up in no time, Ms. Courtney."

That was what she wanted, wasn't it? Better a quick, clean break than protracted negotiations. Lauren looked over the offer, skimming through the fine print. The man's price was more than fair, and his conditions minimal. As she took out her pen and signed the document, Marjorie

heaved a big sigh. "I wish all my sales were that easy.
You wouldn't believe how fussy people can be." She
checked the date on the offer. "You can move out that
quickly?"

"I want this over and done with," Lauren said. "I'll
call the removal firm in a few minutes. Thanks so much,
Marjorie, and I'll talk to you later this afternoon."

Marjorie took the hint and drove away. Lauren unlocked
the front door and walked in. The rooms were awash in
sunlight that had an added clarity from the ocean's near-
ness. Normally the pine floors, pastel walls, and carefully
garnered antiques welcomed Lauren back; but not today.
Wallace's past and her own decisive actions had exiled her
from a house that had always been a refuge and a place
of renewal.

Tears streaking her cheeks, she slowly walked from
room to room, occasionally picking up a knickknack or
running her fingers along a picture frame, saying her private farewells. She was so immersed in this ritual that the
scrunch of tires in the gravel driveway and the slam of a
car door came like a physical intrusion. Then the doorbell
rang.

She could ignore it. But perhaps it was the purchaser,
come to discuss some further details. She swiped at her
cheeks and walked downstairs, her dark green skirt sway-
ing around her knees.

As the door swung open and Reece saw Lauren standing
in the sunlight, his heart gave a great thud in his chest. He
hadn't been at all convinced she'd be here. She looked
very unhappy; then in swift succession shocked, frightened
and aghast. He said, "You sure took off from the yacht
club in a hurry."

He'd planned to sound conciliatory; but the total lack

of welcome in her face infuriated him. Part of his anger, he knew, arose from sheer relief that she was safe. But not all of it.

The color had drained from her cheeks. "Reece?" she whispered, gripping the door frame as though it were all that was holding her up. "What are you doing here? How did you know where to find me?"

"Oh, it wasn't easy. I had all the Vancouver hotels checked, then your studio—no sign of you anywhere. So I thought you might come here, and flew in an hour ago."

"I thought you had to go to London."

"Haven't you heard about delegating?"

"Am I supposed to feel flattered?"

"You've been crying," he said abruptly.

"If I've just had hysterics, it's nothing to do with you."

"It's everything to do with me," he retorted; and listened to the words replay in his head.

"Oh, no, it's not. So why don't you fly right back where you came from and leave me alone?"

"We've got some unfinished business."

"I absolve you—you can publish anything you like about Wallace. What a fool you must have thought me! *But I adore Wallace. I knew him through and through, he'd never do anything dishonest*...well, I've learned my lesson. I couldn't trust Sandor and I shouldn't have trusted Wallace and as for you, you can't get out of my life too soon."

Reece planted one foot firmly on the step so she couldn't slam the door in his face. "The unfinished business has nothing to do with Wallace."

She ignored him, her cheeks now bright as red flags. "As you're here, you can take this. It's a start, at least." And she thrust a piece of paper at him.

He unfolded it. It was a postdated cheque for three hundred thousand dollars, made out to Lauren. "What's this all about?"

"I've just sold the place. Those are the proceeds. I now owe you two hundred thousand, which you'll get as soon as I can sell my studio."

"Are you out of your mind?" he asked in a cracked voice.

"You think I can live with myself knowing my stepfather cheated you out of half a million dollars?"

"You didn't cheat me! He did."

"For years he was the only real family I had. I feel responsible. Or is that a concept you don't understand?"

"Lauren," Reece said strongly, "I don't like standing on the doorstep like an insurance salesman. Let's continue this indoors."

"There's nothing to continue."

She looked as though she meant it. He tugged her fingers free of the door frame, and stepped up so he was level with her, his body very close to hers. The result was entirely predictable: he wanted to take her in his arms and kiss her until she melted in his embrace.

Right. Just like the last time.

Which was, of course, the unfinished business he'd mentioned. However, if he had any sense, he'd wait a few minutes before broaching the subject of sex. She didn't exactly look receptive.

Pushing past her, he looked around in genuine appreciation, feeling the old house welcome him, hearing through an open window the soft rhythms of the sea. "Have you spent a lot of time here over the years?"

She was backed against the wall, her eyes inimical. "When are you going to publish the evidence against Wallace?"

"What makes you think I will?"

"I broke the terms of our agreement."

"So did I. We said no sex."

Her lips tightened. "I'm glad you're not laboring under the delusion that we made love."

"Low blow, Lauren."

"It's the only language you understand."

"Why don't you just come right out and tell me what a rotten bastard I am?" he said pleasantly.

She straightened, jamming her fists in the pockets of her skirt, which swirled around her hips. "You're a destroyer," she said bitterly. "I loved Wallace. I loved this house. If my mother cared about me when I was little, she certainly gave no evidence of doing so as I got older. I don't remember my real father, and my second stepfather couldn't wait for me to leave town. So I put my need for a loving parent onto Wallace, and my search for security into this house. And now you've smashed both of them. Do you destroy everything you touch?"

A bloodstained sidewalk in Chicago... Reece said evenly, "I'll offer the purchaser twice what he paid, and give you the house back."

"Money can't fix everything, Reece." Her voice broke. "Don't you see? I *loved* Wallace. And now I'm left with nothing. With less than nothing, because what I thought I had was false."

The words, unplanned, came from deep within him. "Tell me what you loved about Wallace."

"He was kind, he was fun, he made me laugh. He used to sing old Broadway hits at the top of his lungs and teach me all the lyrics. He did crazy things, like going swimming in April and riding a bicycle in the snow...and he listened to me. Listened and was smart enough not to give advice."

Tears were trickling down her cheeks; she ignored them with total disdain. Knowing better than to touch her, Reece said, "And you think that his dishonest financial dealings have erased all that? People aren't single-faceted, Lauren. Yes, he committed fraud—although like Robin Hood, he only took from the rich. And yes, he was a wonderful stepfather who spent a lot of time with you. One side of his personality doesn't negate the other. You're in danger of throwing out the baby with the bathwater."

She was frowning at him. "I am?"

"Sounds to me as though he gave you much more than he took away from me. Because he gave you what money can't buy. Love and security when you desperately needed both."

"You're right," she said slowly, "he did."

"He was an imperfect human being. Just like the rest of us."

Even more slowly, she said, "When I called you a destroyer, you looked—well, shattered would be one word. What were you thinking about, Reece?"

His throat closed. He couldn't tell her, he'd never talked to anyone about the nightmare scene that had greeted him when he'd come back from the bank machine. His mother, the day before her death eight years ago, had asked him to look after Clea. But Reece had failed and Clea had died.

He came back to himself to realize that Lauren had stepped closer, her hand resting on his sleeve, her face gentled by compassion. "Please tell me."

"I can't," he said in a raw voice.

"You can trust me."

Her eyes, turquoise as the sea that glimmered through the window, were full of pleading. He'd never trusted anyone but Clea with his emotions, he realized with a shock of surprise. And then she'd died and he'd closed down.

Now Lauren was asking him to extend that same trust

o her. "How can I trust you? We've known each other
ess than two weeks."

"We did go to bed together yesterday."

Feeling obscurely angry, he retorted, "It's one thing to
trip my body. Another to strip my soul."

"For me, the two go together."

"For you, maybe."

Compassion, he noticed, had been replaced with what
ould only be called distance. She said flatly, "Then we
ave nothing more to say to each other. When I've cashed
hat cheque, I'll send you another for the full amount. And
vhen I've sold the studio, I'll do the same thing."

"If you put your studio on the market, I'll buy it and
eed it back to you."

"You wouldn't dare!"

"Try me. Nor will I accept any money from this
ouse."

"Reece, I'm trying my best to make amends."

"You don't have to—don't you get it?"

"You just can't accept money from a woman."

"And where will you work if you sell your studio? On
ie street? Show a little common sense, for God's sake."

"I'll rent a space. I'll manage, I always have."

"And what if you're pregnant?" Reece said nastily.
Have you thought of that?"

She paled. "No..."

"Are you on the Pill?"

"Of course not. I told you I hadn't slept with anyone
nce Sandor." Distraught, she added, "It all happened so
ıst, I didn't even think about protection."

"Nor did I. For which I take full responsibility. Don't
ou see, Lauren, we're tied together, we can't just go
ur separate ways. I want to make love to you again, so
ıat—"

"No!"

She'd taken a step backward into a pool of sunlight, her hand warding him off; predominant among the emotions churning in his chest was hurt. He said, "I know I—"

"The bargain's over, I'll send you a cheque and you can give it to a home for stray cats for all I care."

She meant it, he thought sickly. She really didn't want anything more to do with him. Feeling as though he'd been knifed in the ribs, determined not to show he was bleeding, he allowed anger to overwhelm the pain. He was damned if he was going to beg. He'd never had to before, and he wasn't going to start now. Kiss her into submission? No, thanks. If she wasn't willing, to hell with her. He said harshly, "I'll call you in a month or so to find out if you're pregnant. You'd better hope you're not—I'd hate for you to have someone you despise as the father of your child."

The light was shining mercilessly on her face; beneath her anger, she looked strained and stubborn. She couldn't wait to get him out of her life, he thought savagely. But what did he care? He'd never gone where he wasn't wanted, and he wasn't going to change that for a sculptor with enormous talent, tangled hair and a body that obsessed him. "Goodbye, Lauren," he said with formal precision, and without waiting for her to reply, turned and left the house.

This was going to be the shortest car rental in history, he thought, climbing in and driving away. But maybe he'd needed to see Lauren to realize there was nothing there for him. The only connection left between them was a cheque he neither needed nor wanted; and a possible pregnancy whose ramifications he couldn't even begin to contemplate.

Not much for the week they'd spent together.

Painfully little.

But why would he want more?

CHAPTER ELEVEN

LAUREN turned the music up another notch. The studio was crowded, the wine and beer were flowing, and everyone seemed to be having a wonderful time. Except for her.

It was just under a week since Reece had visited her in the house she'd inherited from Wallace. The sale had gone through without a hitch, and yesterday she'd mailed a cheque for three hundred thousand dollars to Reece's London headquarters. She'd sounded out a real estate agent about selling her studio, although something had stopped her from actually putting it on the market. The certainty that Reece would indeed buy it?

The buzzer sounded again; a few moments later Sam walked in the door. He was carrying a bouquet of Calla lilies that he presented to her with a flourish, and a bottle of very good wine. Above the noise, she teased, "Maybe we should hide that in the cupboard, most of this crew have passed the stage where they'd appreciate it. Lovely flowers, thanks."

"They reminded me of miniature sculptures," he said, and kissed her cheek. "Sorry I'm late, I got held up in a meeting. You're looking altogether ravishing."

She was wearing a pencil-slim long skirt with a glittering gilt top that hugged her breasts; her hair was a mass of curls around her face. She was giving the party for two reasons: to celebrate the sale of a major work, and to cheer herself up. She felt far from ravishing; but no one need guess that. "Thank you," she said. "Come along and I'll introduce you to some of my friends."

"How about I dance with you first?" Sam said, dumping the lilies and the wine on the counter and steering her toward the expanse of hardwood floor under the high rafters of her studio. Edging his way through the crowd, he took her in his arms. "Nice to see you…is your stint as Reece's hostess done with?"

Lauren missed a step. "Yes."

Sam looked at her quizzically. "Are you going to tell me what that was all about?"

"I am not."

"He dropped in on our meeting tonight—that's why I was late. He looked like hell."

"You mean he's in the city?" she squawked. "Did you tell him you were coming here?"

"Nope."

"Good," she said with heartfelt gratitude.

"Lauren, Reece is a thoroughly decent guy—even if he does come across as a bit autocratic."

"A bit? He invented the word. Besides, he's completely out of touch with his emotions."

It was Sam's turn to miss a step. "If he is, there are good reasons."

"So tell me what they are."

"He's the only one who can do that."

"I'll be a cranky old woman of ninety-nine before it happens."

"Why don't you just ask him?"

"I have. No dice."

"Try again."

"As I told him I never want to see him again, that might be a little difficult."

"Two autocrats," Sam said dryly.

"I am not!"

"Could have fooled me. By the way, a guy wearing a

purple sarong is letting in more people—that okay with you?''

"My parties always seem to get a bit out of hand...too many starving artists, I guess."

"Hey," said Sam, "guess who's just come in the door?"

Alerted by something in his voice, Lauren jerked her head around. Across the width of the crowded, noisy studio, her eyes met Reece's. Met and clashed, his a blaze of blue. His formal business suit was an interesting contrast to the sarong, she thought faintly, and tried without success to pull her gaze away.

"He looks a touch out of sorts," Sam said cheerfully. "Why don't we go over and say hello?"

Lauren clutched his sleeve. "No way!"

"Lauren, you can have a scene with him in the middle of the dance floor, or you can have it over by the door. Your choice."

"I am not having a scene with Reece Callahan anywhere. Least of all at my party."

"Tell him that."

"Anyway, you don't have to sound so delighted at the prospect of the two of us going at each other tooth and nail."

With sudden seriousness, Sam went on, "You and Reece are made for each other. Although by the looks of it, neither one of you wants to admit it."

"That's the most ridiculous thing I've ever heard."

Sam eased her past a couple so blatantly and blissfully entwined that Lauren averted her eyes, aware of a stab of pure envy. "You're just the woman Reece needs," Sam persisted. "And you're not exactly indifferent to him."

"I'm not indifferent to tarantulas."

Sam laughed, shoving through the melee around the bar.

"Nearly there. I noticed a gorgeous blonde over by the window, I'm going to check her out. But holler if you need me."

"Gee, thanks a lot," Lauren said, and found herself planted in front of Reece. He looked no more pleased to see her than she him. Sam said with infuriating calmness, "Nice to see you, Reece. Women like it when you smile at them, ever notice that?"

"Keep your advice to yourself and why didn't you tell me you were coming here?" Reece said with dangerous softness.

"You didn't ask. See you, Lauren."

Determined to seize the initiative, Lauren said, "Reece, if you came here hoping for a major row or a cozy twosome, you've got the wrong night and the wrong woman."

"Why did Sam bring you over here?"

"Oh, he thinks you and I are made for each other."

A muscle tightened in Reece's jaw. "It's time he took a vacation—his brain's addled."

"So if you don't think we're made for each other, why are you here?"

"Are you pregnant?"

Her lashes flickered. "It's too soon to tell and I don't think you came here to ask that," she retorted. Someone had turned her CD player to top volume; as the party eddied and swirled throughout the studio, she and Reece could have been isolated on a desert island for all the attention they were getting.

Reece shoved his hands in his pockets and said in a raw voice, "I came because I want to make love to you again, Lauren. I'm sorry about the last time—I should never have gone near you at the yacht club knowing my colleagues were waiting in the other room, I must have been out of my mind. But when I saw you with that towel slipping from your breasts, I just plain lost it." He raked his fingers through his hair. "I don't know if any of that makes sense to you, and I don't really expect you to forgive me."

Her temper died. She knew in her bones Reece was being as honest as he knew how; and responded with a matching honesty. "Reece, for my own reasons, I don't want to make love to you again. But thank you for apologizing, I needed that."

"Why don't you want to?" he said hoarsely. "I swear it would be different this time."

She crossed her arms over her chest, her gilt top shimmering in the dim light. She might as well tell him the whole truth; he'd probably guessed it anyway. "I hated sex with Sandor—he called me frigid, and he was right. So the other day in bed with you was simply a confirmation of everything he'd ever told me." She bit her lip. "I couldn't bear to make love with you again—don't you see? I couldn't bear to."

"My God," Reece said softly. "So he did that to you, too?"

"He didn't do it—I was the one with the problem."

"He was totally wrong for you."

"It's so ridiculous that he accused me of promiscuity," she burst out. "Why would I go to bed with other men when everything I'd learned from him told me to steer clear of sex?"

Very gently Reece rested his hands on her shoulders. She flinched from his touch, unable to help herself, and saw his face contract. "Listen to me," he said forcefully. "Remember that kiss in Vancouver? Remember the night I carried you into my bedroom? I know you desired me that night, I saw it, I felt it. We can do that again, we can prove Sandor wrong. Provided you'll trust me."

She shook her head, her eyes downcast. "I'm afraid to."

"I swear I'll be as good to you as I know how. And if at anytime you want to stop, you have only to say so."

Ducking her head, she mumbled, "I'm crying again. I don't know what it is about you, but I'm like a leaky watering can." In sudden defiance she looked up, tears clinging to her lashes. "Anyway, why would you want to do that? Go to bed with a woman who doesn't enjoy sex? Sounds like masochism to me."

"Because I'm ninety-nine percent sure you'll enjoy it with me," he said with a crooked smile that made one tear plop to her cheek. "And if that makes me sound conceited as hell, so be it."

"And what if I do like it?" she cried. "You kiss me goodbye and take off for Cairo on the first flight?"

"Now that I've started delegating, I might just continue."

Panic closed her throat. "I don't know which scares me more—that I'll hate it or I'll love it."

"You've got to trust me, Lauren—that's partly what this is about. The other person you've got to trust is yourself."

The heat from his fingers seeped through the flimsy gilt fabric; the force of his personality beat against her defenses. "Trust goes both ways," she said slowly. "How did your sister die, Reece?"

Involuntarily his nails dug into her shoulders. Then, with a complete absence of emotion, he said, "I left her on the sidewalk in Chicago while I went to a bank machine. She was shot down and robbed. The last thing my mother asked me to do before she died was to look after Clea."

A series of nightmare images flickered through Lauren's brain, vivid, terrible and ineradicable. Instinctively she put her arms around Reece's waist and held him as tightly as she could. "I'm so sorry," she whispered.

"It's five years ago now."

"But you never talk about it."

"What's the point?"

She said intuitively, "Sam knows...doesn't he?"

"Sam was Clea's boyfriend."

So that was why Sam had come so quickly to Reece's defense. "He never told me."

"I asked him not to."

Suddenly exhausted, letting her hands drop to her sides, she said helplessly, "No wonder you shut down your emotions."

He said flatly, "You see why I don't tell people—look how it's upset you."

"That's no reason not to tell me," she flashed.

"It's every reason, I would have thought."

She stated the obvious. "You loved her."

"Oh, for God's sake, Lauren—drop it, will you?"

His eyes were hooded; she knew she'd get nothing more from him about Clea. "So where do we go from here?" she asked with careful restraint.

"Start hiding all the beer in the hopes everyone'll go home," he said promptly. "So we can go to bed with each other."

She gazed up at him. He'd loved Clea and Clea had died. More as a statement than a question, Lauren said, "But you don't love me."

"I want to undo the harm I did at the yacht club— especially now I know the circumstances."

Her decision would change her whole life, Lauren was under no illusions about that. Change it for better or for worse. "I—I've got to pay some attention to this party," she muttered. "Put some food out. Make the coffee."

"So what's your answer?"

He'd removed his hands from her shoulders, as though he scorned to use touch as a weapon to plead his cause.

And he was giving her the chance—as Charlie had said—to rid herself of Sandor once and for all.

But only a chance. Not a certainty.

Under the cover of some astonishingly raucous rap music, Lauren mumbled, "Yes."

"What did you say?"

"Yes—I will," she yelled just as someone turned the music off.

Her words rang under the rafters. Heads turned, a ripple of laughter ran through her guests, and the man in the purple sarong, whose name Lauren had never caught, waved a beer bottle over his head and yelled back, "I've been waiting all evening for you to say that, my darlin'."

The beer bottle arched spray through the air. Purple-sarong gave her a blissful smile, Reece looked murderous, and Lauren swallowed the urge to dissolve into hysterical giggles. Then her friend Daly, a painter of some renown, grabbed her by the waist, perhaps taking pity on her. "I knew you wanted to dance with me," he said, and whirled her onto the dance floor.

"There isn't any music," she muttered.

"We make up our own," Daly said. "Who's the irate gentleman in the Wall Street suit?"

"I couldn't possibly begin to explain," Lauren said. "Daly, have you ever been in love?"

"Dozens of times. Trouble is, I bed 'em and I move on."

"You men are all alike."

"Some of us are worse than others. Sandor was a creep, Lauren. One hundred percent sleaze. Kindly don't put me in the same category as him."

She'd always liked Daly. Wondering with one part of her brain whatever had possessed her to give this party,

Lauren said, "You've been in lust. Not in love. That's what you're saying."

"Yep. I don't know who the guy in the suit is, but he looks about as different from Sandor as you could get. Glad you said yes to him, Lauren—yes to what, by the way?"

"None of your business," she said fractiously. "Do you think if I produced a big pot of very strong coffee my guests would take the hint?"

Daly laughed. "You can try. Want a hand with the grub?"

She gave him something like a genuine smile. "Thanks—you're a real pal."

"Time you came out of that icebox you've been living in," Daly said lightly. "Let's see if I can steer you in the direction of the kitchen."

For the next hour Lauren kept herself extremely busy serving curried meat balls, broiled shrimp and cheese straws, as well as tactfully suggesting coffee to as many of her guests as she could. Reece, to her infinite gratitude, was keeping his distance; although every now and then she'd find him watching her with an intensity that made a shiver race along her spine.

The party started to break up around two in the morning, and by three the last of the stragglers—among them the man in the purple sarong—had gone through the door. Lauren closed it behind him, shoved the bolt across and put the chain in its slot. Was she locking purple-sarong out or herself in? she wondered crazily, and said in a voice that sounded almost normal, "What a mess this place is. But people had a good time, didn't they?"

"Except for you and me," Reece said wryly.

He'd turned the music off. The studio echoed with silence and emptiness. Feeling horribly at sea, she said,

"Half the time I was praying for them to leave and the rest of the time I wanted them to stay all night."

"Let's go to bed, Lauren."

"Shouldn't we clean—"

"I'll help you in the morning."

"It is the morning."

His features a hard mask, Reece rasped, "You're really dreading this, aren't you?"

"Do you want to back out?" she said with a flash of hope.

"No, I don't want to. I'm not going to ask you the same question because I'm pretty sure you'd say yes...let's go upstairs."

Her bedroom and bathroom were in a loft over the studio. "What if Sandor's right?" she said in sudden anguish. "What then?"

"Trust me, Lauren," Reece said forcibly. "That's all you've got to do—trust me."

"That's one heck of a lot," she said with something of her normal spirit.

He laughed. "It sure is. You go first."

The stairway was steep, and her skirt rather tight. Conscious in every nerve of her body of Reece on her heels, Lauren slipped off her shoes and climbed the stairs. Turning at the top, she said, "I need a shower, I won't be—"

"Let's have one together."

"No! No, I won't be long," she said frantically, scuttled to the bathroom and locked the door.

Sanctuary, she thought, gazing at her face in the mirror. She looked scared to death. Petrified. Terrified. Cornered.

Trust me, Reece had said. Trust me and trust yourself.

Which was precisely what she wasn't doing. She wasn't giving herself a chance. Taking a deep breath, Lauren lifted her chin and gazed deep into her own eyes. To the best of her ability, she was going to trust Reece. Trust that he had her best interests at heart.

Because, of course, she had no idea why he was really here. To make amends? Intuitively she knew there was more going on than that. To get in touch with his own emotions, buried with his dead sister? Perhaps that was closer to the truth. Perhaps Reece had his own healing to do. And perhaps she could help him in that.

Somewhat heartened, she stripped off her clothes and showered. Her nightgown was hanging on the hook on the door. It was full-length, made of delicately embossed cotton; she hauled it over her head, dragged a brush through her hair and opened the door.

Reece was sitting on her bed, taking off his socks. His shirt was already slung over the back of her Windsor chair; it shone very white against the taupe walls. He smiled at her. "I'll have a shower, too. Any clean towels?"

"In the cupboard," she said, and watched the muscles ripple across his chest as he stood up. The door closed behind him; her newfound courage seemed to have deserted her. She sat down hard on the other side of the bed, her fingers clasped in her lap, and wondered what Wallace would think were he to see her now. If it hadn't been for his duplicity, she wouldn't be here, waiting for a man who felt like a stranger to make love to her.

All too soon, Reece came back into the bedroom, a towel wrapped around his waist. In a strangled voice, Lauren said, "Put out the light...please?"

As he flicked the switch, the dim glow of the city filtered through the skylight over the bed. Then Reece sat down beside her, taking her hands and chafing them gently between his own. The warmth of his shoulder seeped through the thin cotton of her gown.

She had to go through with it. She had to.

CHAPTER TWELVE

LAUREN'S fingers were ice-cold. And it was up to him to warm them, Reece thought. Warm her fingers and warm her heart. Undo the damage that bastard Sandor had caused her, and free the woman of passion he was convinced lay behind her panic-stricken eyes.

Free her, and what then?

One thing at a time, Reece, he told himself, and brought her hand up to his lips, dropping small kisses along her thumb and the back of her hand, then turning it to bury his face in her palm. Her wrists were as stiff as boards; her rapid, shallow breathing smote him to the heart. Raising his head, he cupped her face and, with infinite gentleness, kissed her on the lips.

Her jaw was rigid, her mouth unresponding, so much so that he wondered if his confidence had been misplaced. Had the damage gone too deep? Or was he quite simply the wrong man for her? Both thoughts filled him with a hollow ache of emptiness he didn't want to analyze.

With exquisite control, he moved his mouth over hers; and felt the first tentative softening of her lips. He said softly, "Lauren, my beautiful Lauren...I'm so happy to be here with you," and with a small shock of surprise knew his words to be the truth. He wanted her body, no question of that. But more than that, he wanted her presence.

He took her lower lip between his teeth, nibbling its soft curve, letting his tongue brush her mouth with tantalizing brevity. As she made a tiny sound deep in her throat, he put his arms around her, stroking the taut line of her shoul-

ders with repetitive smoothness. His own body was in no
doubt of what it wanted. Slow down, Reece. This is for
Lauren. Not for you.

Then her hands slid up his torso and linked themselves
behind his neck. Her breath wafted his cheek in a small
sigh. "Reece, I..."

"Tell me what you want, sweetheart. I'll do anything I
can for you."

Briefly she burrowed her face into his bare shoulder, her
sweetly scented hair falling to his chest; then she looked
right at him. "I don't know what I want...show me what
I want, Reece. Please?"

His heart pounding like a triphammer, he bent to kiss
her again, this time unleashing some of his desire; after a
fractional hesitation, he felt her match him kiss for kiss,
her lips parting to the dart of his tongue, her own tongue
playing with his. Wondering if his heart could burst in his
chest, Reece fought for control. He mustn't rush her. He'd
done that once. Never again.

He kissed her lips, the hollow of her cheekbone, the
sweep of her forehead; then let his mouth drift down her
throat to the pulse where the beat of her blood told its own
story. He fumbled for the buttons on her gown, saying with
a thread of laughter, "These things weren't invented with
me in mind."

She said shyly, "I could take it off."

Shaken to the core, he said, "You're so full of courage."

"I want you to make love to me," she whispered.

His hands unsteady, he helped her lift the soft folds of
cotton over her head. Her creamy skin gleamed in the soft
light; her full breasts, her curve of waist and hip, struck
him dumb. He felt as though he'd never made love to a

woman before. He felt as though he'd been given an immeasurable gift that he in no way deserved.

Teasing her nipples to hardness, he watched her eyes darken, heard her breathing quicken in her throat. Suddenly she took his face between her hands, kissing him with an unbridled fierceness that took his breath away. He drew her down beside him on the bed, feeling the towel slip from his waist; and again had to draw on all his willpower to subdue his body's tumultuous response.

Wanting only to give her pleasure, he caressed her breasts until she whimpered with need, her body arching so that the softness of her skin rubbed against his body hair. Her eyes were dazed with wonderment; very slowly, he drew one hand down her belly, seeking out the soft, damp crevice between her thighs. She gave a single, sharp cry, moving her hips against his with an unpracticed seductiveness that told Reece more than he needed to know about Sandor's selfishness and her essential innocence. He dropped his face to her belly, rejoicing in the smoothness of her skin, then moved downward, parting her thighs, his tongue plummeting to give her the pleasure she'd been denied; yet stopping before she could topple over the edge.

In a broken voice he'd never heard before, she gasped, "Reece, oh, Reece…I've never felt like this in my life. So overcome, so frantic."

He touched her where she was most sensitive, watching her features convulse. As she cried out his name, he hurriedly reached for the little package by the bed; then he slid into her, moving as slowly as he could, until he thought he'd die from the pain of holding back. Not until she was begging him for more did he plunge into her. Thrusting in and out, he waited until she was shuddering with the inexorable rhythms of surrender before allowing himself to meet her in that place where he was most alive and most intimately joined to her.

A new place, Reece thought dazedly. Depths he'd never plumbed. A union unlike any other.

Very slowly, he lowered his body to hers, feeling against his ribs the frantic racing of her heart, her dazzled face only inches from his. "Lauren," he muttered, "are you all right?"

She opened her eyes. Brilliantly turquoise, they smiled up at him. "All right? I'm overwhelmed, I've come home, I—I just never knew..." Then suddenly she clutched him to her and began to weep, her face buried against his throat.

He held her hard, rolling over on his side so his weight wouldn't crush her, feeling her sobs shaking her frame. "Was I too fast for you? I didn't—"

She looked right at him, her breath still heaving in her chest. "You were perfect—I wanted you so badly. But I must have been clumsy, I'm sorry if—"

He began to laugh, hugging her to him and inhaling the lilac scent of her hair; and knowing he'd never felt as close to a woman as he did to Lauren now. "No more apologies. I think we both did just fine, how about that?"

Her cheeks pink, she said, "We did, didn't we?"

"Next time," he said deliberately, "we'll do even better."

"How long do I have to wait?" she asked saucily.

"Not as long as you might think."

As she blushed entrancingly, he drew one hand down the length of her body. He was exactly where he'd wanted to be ever since she'd walked into his Vancouver office that day in her severe gray suit: in Lauren's bed. Learning about her. Discovering her vulnerabilities and her incredible courage, her laughter and her newly released passion.

Passion whose subtleties they'd only just begun to explore. He thrust his hands into the soft weight of her hair, drawing her face to his and kissing her as though they'd never made love, as though she were utterly new to him and all the more needing to be wooed.

"You're my heart's desire," he said roughly, and heard the words echo in his mind. He wasn't in love with her. Of course not. He wanted her, that was all. Wanted her more than he'd ever wanted anyone or anything in his life.

With all his powers of imagination and empathy, Reece set about showing Lauren just how much he wanted her; he was rewarded, as the first light of dawn streaked the sky, by a mutual release that overpowered him in its intensity. He lay on top of her, sweat filming his forehead, his heartbeat like a drumroll in his chest, and wondered how he was ever going to say goodbye to her.

He had to go to London the day after tomorrow. No choice.

Two more days, he thought, letting his cheek rest on her hair, feeling through every nerve ending the sweet clasp of her arms around his ribs. That'll be enough. We're both adults, with full lives, and this is a temporary madness. We'll be fine. Of course we will be.

The shrilling of the telephone woke Lauren from a deep sleep. With a jolt she realized a man's body was curled around her, one arm heavy over her hips, one thigh pinioning her to the mattress. Reece. With whom she'd made love twice through the night, discovering within herself a woman she hadn't known existed.

She rolled over, grabbed the receiver and mumbled, "Hello," only to be greeted by the dial tone and the continued peal of a telephone bell.

Reece sat up beside her. "It's my cell phone," he muttered. "Where did I put my jacket?"

He scrambled out of bed, lunged for his jacket and took the phone from the pocket. "Hello," he barked. Then he said nothing for several minutes.

His body, so lean and strongly muscled, was utterly beautiful, Lauren thought. She wouldn't sculpt him, though. Not yet. Not until he was so much a part of her that she wouldn't even need to see him for her hands to trace his outlines.

She wanted him again. Wanted him fiercely and now. Half appalled, half amused by her own reactions, so delicious and so surprising, she realized Reece was now talking. Abruptly her heart grew cold, as she heard him say, "Gary, I can't believe this has happened. So much for thinking we were on top of it. Okay, I'll leave as soon as I can. But I can't possibly arrive before midafternoon—at least the jet's at Kennedy, so there won't be a holdup there. You'll meet me at Heathrow? Fine, I'll get the pilot to radio ahead. 'Bye.''

Without even looking at Lauren, he quickly entered some numbers. "Randolph? I'll need the limo in fifteen minutes." Giving Lauren's address, he went on, "Kennedy Airport, yeah. You'll call Tom and alert the crew we'll need to head for London as soon as possible? Thanks." Then he jammed the phone back in his pocket and turned to face Lauren.

"You must have heard that. I've got to go to London, pronto. A major deal could fall apart unless I get over there and do some damage control—it's something we've been working on the last four months. And I'm the only one to handle it."

Her smile had congealed; aware that she was cold, she

grabbed at the sheet, pulling it up to hide her nakedness. In a stony voice, she said, "Go ahead."

"I'd never have anticipated this," he exploded, "I thought Gary and I had covered all the angles—but I was wrong. I'm not going to London because I want to—I'm going because I have to. I want to be here with you, surely you know that?"

"Of course," she said politely.

He pulled her to her feet, his hands clasping her shoulders. The sheet slipped down her body; she clutched at it, feeling exposed and vulnerable. He said urgently, "Lauren, last night was—I can't begin to tell you how wonderful it was. Listen to me, will you? This business shouldn't take more than a week maximum, then I'll come right back here. Before I go to Cairo."

"You'd better get dressed," she said. "Your driver will be here in a few minutes."

"You're not listening to me! I know the timing's lousy. But it's not the end of the world...I'll be back, do you hear me?"

"If I want you back," Lauren said.

"Oh, you want me," he said furiously, pulling her toward him and kissing her with such passionate hunger that her body ached with desire even as her soul was filled with a fierce resentment that he should leave so precipitously. Although why should she be surprised? He'd never married, he must be an expert at extricating himself from women's beds.

She pulled her head free. "Don't, Reece! You don't have to pretend. Or lie. I'm sure I'm an amateur compared to your other lovers, so why would you want to stay?"

His breath hissed between his teeth. "Are you accusing me of setting this up? As a way—an extraordinarily graceless way—of dumping you?"

"Why wouldn't I? I'm no sexual gymnast, no sophisticated jet-setter who's read all the manuals. I behaved like a virgin. Not your type."

"Why don't you let me decide who's my type—as you so cold-bloodedly put it? Are you also saying if I come back here in a week, you won't let me in?"

"It's all happened too fast," she cried, pressing her palms to her cheeks in unconscious drama. "Last night I—I was transported. And now you're leaving. Going four thousand miles away. How am I supposed to behave? Wave my handkerchief at the window and shed a few decorative tears?"

His crooked grin relieving some of the tension in his face, Reece said, "I have difficulty with that picture—you're more likely to take a sledgehammer to my forehead. Don't you see, Lauren? This is about trust, too. I wouldn't leave here for anything less than a real emergency—you've got to believe me. Because it's true."

She twisted a fold of the sheet between her fingers. "I—I guess I'll let you in," she muttered. "If you come back."

"I've said I will…I'll call you in a couple of days and let you know how things are going. Now I'd better get in the shower and get out of here."

Grabbing his clothes, he headed for the bathroom. Lauren quickly dressed in black pants and a loose mohair sweater, needing the protection that clothing offered. Could she trust Reece? Or was she being an utter fool? Once he'd left, wouldn't he realize he'd had enough of her? After all, he'd more than made amends for events at the yacht club. He'd given her pleasure and fulfillment beyond her wildest imaginings, and hadn't that been his aim?

Why would he bother to come back? He certainly wasn't in love with her, that wasn't part of his life plan.

She brushed her hair, put on earrings and lipstick and went downstairs. The studio looked even messier than it had before she had gone to bed. She ground some coffee and plugged in her espresso machine, trying to keep her mind on what she was doing. Someone had spilled red wine over the counter, and someone else had trodden two shrimps into the hardwood floor. Although Sam's bottle of wine had been drained, the Calla lilies had been stuck in water in a biscuit jar. She found a vase in the cupboard, sliced their stems and was arranging them when Reece came running down the stairs, doing up his cuff links on the way. He said, "I didn't set up that phone call to get out of helping you clean up this mess, either. Those are nice flowers," he added.

"Sam gave them to me."

His lips narrowed. "You planning on falling in love with Sam?"

"I'm not planning on falling in love with anyone," she said sharply. "What about you?"

"Same. Tell me what your favorite flowers are."

"Lilacs. The purple ones with the gorgeous smell."

"Randolph's outside, I've got to go. Look at me, Lauren."

Reluctantly she raised her eyes to his face. His hair was still damp, his eyes very blue. He said strongly, "When I said how wonderful last night was, I was telling the exact truth. And no, it's not my standard line when I say good-bye. *You* were wonderful...so passionate, you took my breath away. In an ideal world, I'd be staying right here and making love to you the whole day through."

Trust me. That's what he was saying. "I—it was wonderful for me, too, Reece." Impetuously she stood on tiptoe and kissed him on the mouth, feeling the contact rip through all her defenses. "Have a safe journey," she quavered.

Cupping her chin, he kissed her thoroughly and at length; her cheeks were as red as her sweater when he stepped back. "Talk to you soon," he said, unlatched her door and was gone.

Lauren stood very still. The studio was distressingly, horribly empty. Why hadn't she hugged him? Why hadn't she told him he'd been incredibly generous last night? That she'd loved his body and everything he'd done upstairs in her bed?

It was too late now. He'd gone.

But she'd see him again soon, she thought stoutly, reaching in the cupboard for a coffee mug and discovering they were all dirty. Of course she would.

He'd said so.

CHAPTER THIRTEEN

THE day Reece left passed fairly quickly, because Lauren was busy washing dishes, lugging down the garbage, and scrubbing the floor. She went to bed very tired, certain that she'd sleep; and as soon as her head touched the pillow was achingly aware of the elusive scent of Reece's body, and of the empty expanse of sheets. She was alone in her bed; except for last night, she'd been alone in her bed for years. But last night had changed everything.

She tried recounting the names of all the people at the party, those she'd invited and those she hadn't; she composed a mental letter to her gallery about her next show; she stared at the rectangle of clouds through the skylight. She felt as though she'd been invaded, as though Reece had flowed through her veins, and was now a denizen of her heart. She was no longer complete, she thought miserably. In just a few hours in her bed, Reece had stolen her hard-earned peace and security.

Why had she ever opened her body to a man who had a business empire that spanned the globe and a heart guarded against both vulnerability and love? She was entirely capable of reading between the lines: the tragic death of his sister had killed something in Reece. He might desire Lauren, but he wouldn't fall in love with her.

She should have sent him away the moment he had walked in her door.

Eventually she did fall asleep. The next day she focused on business matters, visiting her gallery, paying bills and doing some shopping. When she went to bed at eleven, she fell asleep right away; then woke at three in the morning longing for Reece to be beside her.

He should phone today. Who knows, maybe he'd be knocking at her door by nightfall, she thought.

Somewhat comforted, she drifted off to sleep again. The next morning she found out she wasn't pregnant, a bittersweet discovery even though reason told her the last thing in the world she needed was to bear Reece's child. The hours of the day dragged by, her back ached, and by five that afternoon she was battling true panic because she couldn't concentrate on her work, so anxious was she for the phone to ring. Work had always been her refuge; what if she lost even that?

Then the phone did ring, three times in succession: Sam inviting her to a movie, purple-sarong inviting her to go camping, a research company inviting her to answer a survey. She declined them all with varying degrees of politeness, and was alternately enraged and despairing that her peace of mind could be so dependent upon a phone call.

At seven-ten, when she'd almost given up hope, the telephone shrilled. She grabbed the receiver and said breathlessly, "Hello?"

"Lauren? Is that you?"

"Reece—where are you?"

"Heathrow. Again." As her heart leaped with joy that he was on his way to New York, he went on, "Did you listen to the news tonight?"

She hadn't. She'd been too preoccupied with cramps, the clumsiness of her fingers and the recalcitrance of the sheet metal she was working with. "Why? What's up?"

"I've got to go to Ecuador. Three of my staff were taken hostage last night. I've hired some professional negotiators to deal with the ransom, but I have to be there, too. Partly for moral support for the three guys that are prisoners, partly to do my own share of the negotiations.''

His voice was clipped and emotionless. "How long do you think it'll take?'' she asked, trying to sound just as composed.

"I've no idea. Sometimes these things are settled right away, sometimes they drag on for weeks...I'd have phoned you sooner, but Gary and I have been working around the clock on that deal that nearly fell through. Lauren, I'm sorry, I know this isn't what I promised, but I couldn't live with myself if I didn't go down there and see for myself what's going on.''

"You'll be careful, Reece?''

"Of course I will,'' he said impatiently.

He was a very rich man; he'd be a prime candidate for being held to ransom himself. All the horror stories she'd ever read in the news flooded her mind; her heart felt like a lump of ice in her breast. "Please look after yourself,'' she begged.

There was a small silence. "You really care?''

This time it was she who was silent. "I—of course I care what happens to you, I wouldn't want anyone to fall in the hands of kidnappers.''

"I see,'' he said with a trace of grimness. "I can't promise how often I'll be in touch, as I'm not sure what conditions will be like down there. But I'll come back as soon as I can, that I do promise. Do you know yet whether you're pregnant?''

"I'm not.''

"Good,'' Reece said. "Neither of us needs that complication.''

Suddenly furious, she retorted, "Heavens, no. A baby? In your perfectly controlled life? Way too messy.''

"Give it a rest, Lauren.''

"Oh, pardon me," she snapped. Her fingers tightened around the receiver: a piece of plastic that was her only connection to Reece before he disappeared into dangers all the more threatening for being unknown. Appalled, she said raggedly, "Reece, I'm sorry. My back hurts, I haven't been able to settle down and work since you left, I'm hardly sleeping—I don't want you to go to Ecuador thinking I'm angry with you."

"If it's any help, I'm not sleeping, either." His voice deepened. "All I can think of is the softness of your skin, your beauty, the way you responded to me…I'll be back as soon as I can, I swear."

"I'll look forward to seeing you," she said. It was the truth, wasn't it? Although the words seemed hopelessly inadequate to express the storm of emotion in her breast.

"I've got to go—the jet's waiting. Take care of yourself, and if I can't phone you myself, I'll get someone in my London office to keep in touch."

"Thank you…'bye," she whispered.

The connection was cut. Slowly Lauren put down the phone and looked around the studio as though she'd never seen it before. A man with piercing blue eyes had severed her from a life she'd painstakingly rebuilt in the years after Sandor. A life in which she'd been more than content.

She couldn't go back. The past was just that: the past. And the future was so clouded with uncertainties that there was no refuge for her there, either.

Work, she thought. I'll work until I drop and I'll sleep the rest of the time. And who knows, Reece may be back in only a few days.

The days dragged by, and turned into weeks. November became December. Punctiliously every third day a man called Ross phoned Lauren from London to report on the negotiations, at first on their total lack of progress because of the outrageous demands of the hostage takers, and later on the inch-by-inch concessions being made by both sides. This was normal, he assured Lauren. She shouldn't worry, every precaution was being taken to insure the safety of the negotiating team.

Reece himself phoned four times, the connections so bad that Lauren could scarcely hear him. He sounded tired and frustrated, deeply worried about the safety of his employees, yet unable to accede to the demands of the kidnappers because to do so would have endangered the lives of local inhabitants. Lauren had never felt so helpless in her life; helpless and horribly lonely. As a result she threw herself into her work, staying up half the night for two weeks in a row, and producing a massive sculpture in steel and wood that far surpassed anything she'd ever done and that left her exhausted.

Besides talking long-distance to Charlie every week, the other thing she did was see a lot of Sam. He was involved in a project in New York, and was more than happy to drop in for coffee or go to a movie with her. Over a leisurely meal in a little bistro in Greenwich Village, he started talking about Clea, painting a picture of an intelligent, high-spirited young woman whom Sam had adored, and who had loved her brother Reece deeply. "Reece was devastated by her death...I don't think he's ever got over it. I'd never known him to be in love with any of the women he dated, but after Clea, he was like a block of ice." Sam buttered a slice of baguette, his thin face abstracted. "Part of me will always love Clea, and I know in my bones we'd have been happy together. But she's dead, Lauren. She won't be back...and now I've met someone else, in Boston."

"Someone nice?" Lauren ventured.

Sam grinned. "Bright and gorgeous and plays a mean game of tennis." Abruptly he sobered. "I haven't dared tell Reece. I'm afraid he'll think I've abandoned Clea. I'll never abandon her in one sense. But life moves on, and I want a wife and children and a house in the suburbs, all the normal stuff for a guy my age."

"I think you should tell him. When he comes back."

"And who knows when that'll be."

"It's got to be soon," Lauren cried.

"For someone who swears she's not in love, you're sure behaving like you are."

"I'm not! I won't let myself be. Because you're right, Reece took his heart and put it in the deep freeze and it'd take more than me to haul it out of there. So why would I be so stupid as to fall in love with him?"

"Then you both miss out."

"You're a born romantic, Sam."

"Guess you're right." He twirled his linguine around his fork. "Did I ever tell you about Reece's country place in Provence?"

Lauren settled back to listen; she loved hearing stories about Reece, about a younger, happier Reece; it all added to the emerging portrait of a complex man who'd loved his family and was now driven by demons she'd do anything to exorcise. As she went to bed that night, she added to the puzzle the fact that Reece had returned the cheque she'd sent him; nor had he published one word about Wallace.

The next day she went to the library, and on microfiche read the newspaper accounts about Clea's murder on a sidewalk in Chicago one hot summer day. There were photographs, all too graphic, engraving themselves on Lauren's brain. The ones of Reece made her flinch, so haggard, so ravaged did he look; so utterly alone, no matter that he was surrounded by people.

She didn't take any notes; she didn't need to. Her spirit heavy, she left the library and walked home. For ten days she worked, like a woman driven, on a small bronze of two figures, a Pietà in reverse, for the man was holding the woman's body. Then, after a certain amount of research, she mailed a cheque for the exact amount of the sale of her house to an organization in Chicago that worked with street kids. If—when—she saw Reece again, she'd tell him what she'd done.

Of course she'd see him. He'd promised she would.

But there were times, especially in the middle of the night when she woke to an unshared bed, that Lauren doubted this. She lost weight, her eyes looked shadowed, and the next piece she embarked on carried her to even darker territory in her unconscious, places she'd never been before. Charlie told her to throw the key to her studio in the Hudson River. Sam lectured her about vitamins and taking a holiday. Even purple-sarong, when she met him one day on Forty-second Street wearing a pair of perfectly respectable jeans, told her to book a flight to a beach in Baja.

She couldn't. She had to be home to get the snippets of information that were all that connected her to Reece; she needed the security of friends and familiar surroundings. And then one day in mid-December, when the shops were full of Christmas decorations that seemed to mock her unhappiness, the telephone rang.

She was expecting a call from her agent. "Lauren Courtney," she said crisply.

"I'm back in London."

She would have known that voice anywhere. She sat

down hard on the nearest chair. "Reece?" she faltered. "You're home? You're safe?"

"Yes, yes, and yes." His voice altered. "You okay?"

"I never c-cry," she gulped, swiping at the tears that were streaming down her cheeks.

"I thought you'd be happy."

"I am—oh, I am."

"We got in a couple of hours ago. The families of the three guys who were released were all at the airport...the men'll need psychiatric assessments, but I think they'll be fine now that they're home."

"So they were all released?"

He gave her some of the details, none of which she remembered afterward because she was too busy trying to overcome a maelstrom of emotion. Reece was safe. In London. Safe.

"You still there?" he said finally; she could almost see his crooked grin.

"Yes."

"You're being awfully quiet." She didn't know what to say; that was one reason. He went on, "I've got a ton of stuff to catch up on over here. I wondered...would you consider coming over for Christmas? Spending it with me in Surrey? I have a place there that I think you'd like."

"Just you and me?"

"Along with the housekeeper and the groundsman."

"I—I don't know that I'd get a flight this late."

"I'll look after that, I've got connections. Are you saying you don't want to come?" His voice was unreadable.

"You really want me there?"

"I wouldn't be asking you if I didn't."

"All right," she said in a rush. "I'll come."

"How about the twenty-third? We can drive down to Surrey that afternoon."

Ten more days, she thought. How will I last that long? "That sounds fine," she said. "Although there's one condition, Reece."

"Yes?" he said guardedly.

"We give each other one gift only, costing under twenty-five dollars and handmade."

He began to laugh. "That's fine for you. I'm the original clown when it comes to making anything other than hard cash."

"It doesn't have to be fancy."

"This some kind of test?"

"Sometimes money makes things too easy."

"You're so different from anyone else I know," Reece said vigorously. "But if this is what it takes to get you here, then I agree." He hesitated. "How are you, Lauren?"

He didn't mean that in the usual way; he really wanted to know. She said with careful accuracy, "Tired. Confused. So happy you're safe." Taking her courage in her hands, she added shyly, "Wanting very much to go to bed with you again."

"I can't tell you how I'm longing to hold you in my arms."

She gave a breathless laugh. "Ten days isn't long."

"Ten days sounds like forever."

Her whole body felt as though it were on fire. "I think we'll have a very happy Christmas," she said.

"I think you may be right. Lauren, I should go, I've got a million things to see to. I'll call you in a couple of days with all the arrangements. Take care, won't you?"

"You, too," she said. "'Bye, Reece."

As she put down the receiver, she was smiling. Impulsively she turned on the radio and to the strains of Bing Crosby began to dance around her studio floor, imagining that Reece was with her, holding her in his arms just as he'd said he longed to do.

Heaven, she thought. Sheer heaven.

Christmas with Reece. What other gift could she possibly want?

CHAPTER FOURTEEN

REECE was half an hour early at the airport on the twenty-
third. He was never early for appointments, his time was
too valuable for that. So why was he standing in the
crowded arrivals area watching a clock change its digital
numbers with agonizing slowness? Not, as Lauren would
have said, his style.

Lauren. Would they recapture the passion, the intimacy
they'd shared in her loft bedroom? Or was that a once-in-
a-lifetime closeness, destined never to be repeated? And
why did he care so much about the answer to his own
questions?

What was she to him, this woman with hair like sunlight
on copper, and a body that lacerated all his senses? She
was as far from complaisant as a woman could be; she'd
challenged his ingenuity for her Christmas present; and he
was desperate to possess her again.

He hadn't allowed himself to feel remotely like this in
the last five years. Not even before that, if he were honest.
He'd never permitted a woman to arouse him to such ex-
tremities of emotion; hadn't wanted to. Which had had
nothing at all to do with Clea and everything to do with a
growing cynicism about the power of his own fortune.

He took out a financial magazine and tried to concentrate. Slowly the red numbers on the clock changed, until,
over the heads of the crowd, he saw a tall woman with
turquoise eyes hesitating at the barrier. He lifted the bouquet he'd been clutching, waving the great sheaf of lilacs
over his head; and watched her face break into laughter.

She edged her way through the crowd toward him. She was wearing a dramatic long cape of loden green; as she finally reached him, he said, "This isn't your Christmas present. It's a welcome-to-England present."

Her eyes dancing, she said, "Where on earth did you get lilacs at this time of year?"

"It wasn't easy...hello, Lauren."

Her cheeks were flushed; she looked uncertain, happy and shy all at the same time. He leaned over and kissed her on the lips, and as his heart rocketed in his chest, murmured against her mouth, "Do you have any idea how much I want you?"

"I'm not sure this is the place for me to find out."

"You're probably right. Let's go find your luggage."

He tucked her arm in his, covering her fingers with his own, and realized with a jolt of surprise how happy he was. The same kind of feeling he'd had as a little boy, waking up one Christmas morning and finding Santa had brought him the model yacht he'd craved.

He was a big boy now and this was certainly the woman he craved. Should he be reminding himself that he'd out-grown the model by the following Christmas?

To hell with it, thought Reece, and said deliberately, "I thought of taking you to a hotel in the city. First. Then driving to Surrey afterward."

Her blush deepened. "So why aren't you?"

"I guess I'd like us to settle in. In the country."

"I'd like the same. I love Manhattan, but trees and fields sound really good to me right now."

He let his eyes roam her face, simultaneously so familiar and so unknown. "You look tired," he said slowly.

"You mean all that very expensive makeup I splurged on two days ago hasn't done its job?"

"Why so tired, Lauren?"

She hesitated. "If I said the Christmas rush or jet lag, it would be only partly true. Basically, I found the time you were in Ecuador so long that I worked like a madwoman the whole time. Night and day. If it's any consolation, I did three pieces that are probably the best I've ever done. My agent was really bugging me before I left— she's got potential buyers lined up already, but I couldn't deal with the commercial end of it yet. Wasn't ready."

As always, Reece found himself oddly exhilarated by her honesty. Later, when they were alone, he'd ask her more about the three works she'd produced; and knew he'd like to see them. To buy them? He said impulsively, "I didn't really buy those bronze pieces of yours as an investment. There was something about them—I can't explain, but it was as though you knew me. Knew something very important about me...I certainly wasn't going to tell you that on the first day we met."

Someone jostled her, thrusting her against Reece's chest. As his arms automatically went around her, the lilacs sprinkled her cape with tiny mauve blossoms. "Thank you for telling me now," she said softly.

The feel of her body so close to his was driving him out of his mind. "Let's get out of here. I want to be alone with you."

"You really are glad to see me?"

Surprised that she should have to ask, he said, "Of course, isn't it obvious?"

"I don't take anything for granted where you're concerned."

"That, darling Lauren, you can take for granted," he said, and watched her smile glimmer in her eyes. As they claimed her luggage, inched their way out of the city and drove steadily nearer his country estate, Reece found they had plenty to talk about. He described the excruciating weeks he'd spent in Ecuador, she told him about a play she'd seen, they discussed movies and books; as always, he was intrigued by her often unique way of looking at things, and by the play of expression on her face.

Finally they turned into the driveway of his estate. Dusk was falling; as the huge Queen Anne house loomed into view, he saw Lauren's eyes widen. He said awkwardly, "We could stay in the big house, if you'd like. But I thought you might prefer the lodge, it's more comfortable."

He turned down the lane, which was overhung with the bare branches of beech and ash; the lodge, made of stone with a slate roof, had a wreath hanging beside the oak door, and golden light streaming a welcome from the lead-paned windows. Lauren let out her breath in a small sigh. "I like this much better."

"I thought you would. The big house is fine for impressing all the right people—but not for day-to-day living. Hazel, the housekeeper, said she'd leave dinner ready for us. You must be hungry...I'll get your suitcase, if you'll take the lilacs."

He was talking too much. Because he was as excited as a child at Christmas? Because he very much wanted her to like the house that of all the properties he owned was his favorite? He took out the key and unlocked the front door, catching a tang of pine from the wreath along with the subtle, delicate scent Lauren was using. What he mustn't do was fall on her as if he was the one who'd just been released by kidnappers.

The hallway was decorated with holly and mistletoe, its burnished oak paneling reflecting the light from an intricate pewter chandelier. Reece led the way into the living room, where a fire was laid in the hearth. A fir tree was standing in the corner, with a cardboard box beside it; what had seemed a fine idea yesterday now seemed merely sentimental. He said clumsily, "I'm hoping you'll help me decorate the tree tomorrow, that's why I asked Hazel to leave it."

She clasped her hands in delight, like a child. "I'd love to! What a welcoming room, Reece."

He'd always loved its crowded bookshelves and old-fashioned chintz-covered furniture. "The windows overlook the garden. The Christmas roses are in bloom," he said. "Here, let me take your cape and hang it up. And I'd better find some water for those lilacs, they're dropping blossom all over the carpet."

She said suddenly, "If I didn't know better, I'd say you were nervous."

She'd hit altogether too close to home. "I'll put some soup on, too," he said. "What is it, ten-thirty at night to you?"

Lauren lifted her chin. "I don't want any soup. Let's put the lilacs in water and go to bed."

For all her brave talk, her hands were clasped so tightly around the woody stems that her knuckles were white. Flooded by an emotion he couldn't have named, an emotion totally new to him, Reece said huskily, "You're a beautiful woman in all senses of the word. And I agree, bed is where we need to be. Here, give me the lilacs."

But she held on to them. "I'll come with you."

In the kitchen, Reece shoved the flowers in a silver bucket, added water and dumped them on the counter. Lauren said stubbornly, "I want them in the bedroom, they're such a lovely present."

So he lugged the bucket up the narrow staircase and across the hall. The master bedroom also overlooked the garden and the magnificent oaks that sheltered the lodge from the main house. The fireplace was a Victorian addition with a charming metal grate; the bed, canopied, seemed to his overactive imagination to dominate the room. He put the lilacs in the corner. "Would you like me to light the fire?"

"Yes, please...and I'd like a hot bath. Travel always makes me feel scruffy."

"The bathroom's through that door," he said, kneeling to touch a match to the twisted papers in the grate.

By the time flames were leaping up the chimney and he'd lit some candles, he could hear water running in the bathroom. He hung up his coat and suit jacket. Lauren was here, he thought. Here with him for at least a week, just the two of them. No CEOs, no partygoers in purple sarongs, no kidnappers. And, despite his raging hunger for her, no need to rush.

He sat down on the bed, unlacing his shoes and pulling off his socks. "Want me to scrub your back?" he called, tossing his tie over the nearest chair.

Above the splash of water, he heard her laugh. "Sure," she said, "just as long as you're wearing the same amount of clothing as I am."

Grinning to himself, Reece stripped off the rest of his clothes and walked into the bathroom, a room he had insisted be thoroughly modernized. Lauren smiled up at him; although she'd been generous with the water, her breasts were fully exposed, gleaming wetly in the flickering light. His response was instant and unmistakable. She said wickedly, "Guess I shouldn't linger."

He knelt by the tub. She'd piled her hair on her head, exposing the fragile line of her nape. Taking her face in his hands, Reece kissed her with all the pent-up hunger of the weeks they'd been apart. As she kissed him back with an abandon that set his pulses racing, he ran his hands over her body, rediscovering the gentle jut of her bones, rejoicing in her slippery skin. "Come to bed with me, Lauren—now," he said, grasping her wrists and pulling her upright.

She stepped, dripping, onto the mat. He took a towel from the heated rack and wrapped it around her, smoothing it over her curves. Had he ever felt so alive, so certain he was exactly where he needed to be? Then Lauren lifted her face to his, a face blind with hunger. He kissed her, thrusting with his tongue. The towel dropped to the floor.

He was never quite sure how they got from the bathroom to the bedroom, where flames danced on the ceiling and the bed was waiting for them. But somehow she was lying under him, the softness of her breasts and her fierce kisses inflaming his senses until he wondered how his heart could be confined in his chest, so loudly was it pounding. Her hands were everywhere, her breathing as rapid as a bird's, her small, broken cries of rapture like music to his ears. He did his best to hold back, to give her all the pleasure he was capable of, tangling his hands in her hair, laving her nipples, stroking the wet petals between her thighs as she writhed beneath him, her every movement driving him closer and closer to the brink.

And then she toppled, crying out his name in a climactic blend of pain and pleasure that carried him with her. He fell on top of her, throbbing deep inside her, his breath rasping her skin. He was both drained and filled, he thought dazedly, both prisoner and freed. Burying his face in her hair, Reece closed his eyes.

Her arms were wrapped around him, her heart rate gradually slowing. She smelled delicious. He said huskily, "Happy Christmas, Lauren."

She chuckled. "So was that my present?"

"Nope. You don't get that until the twenty-fifth."

"It felt like a present." She stretched luxuriously, her

eyes like deep pools of light. "A wonderful present. Not sure you can surpass it."

"Wait ten minutes," he said, lazily drawing one finger along the rise of her breast.

Her nipple hardened. Trying to look severe, she said, "Ten minutes is a very long time."

"We can always improvise in the meantime," he drawled, leaning over to lick her creamy skin.

"Oh, Reece, I'm so happy to be with you!"

She looked happy. She also looked fulfilled, sensuous, and so beautiful that he had difficulty getting the words out. "I'm happy to be with you, too," he muttered, and knew he'd had enough of words. He began kissing her, taking his time, exploring the planes of her face and the long column of her throat before moving lower, always giving her time for her own responses, which were, he realized with a catch in his throat, growing bolder and more confident every time they made love.

Perhaps that was the real gift he'd given her, Reece thought with a humility new to him. And then stopped thinking altogether as he was caught up in a storm of passion, its rhythms as old as time. Losing himself, drowning in her heat and urgency, he let go of the last vestige of his control and heard his own hoarse cry of satiation echo in his ears.

Panting, he lowered his body to lie beside her, holding her close, never wanting to let her go. Because how would he ever have enough of her? How could he? She completed him as he'd never before been completed.

Was that love?

How would he know? As an adult, he'd never been in love.

Finding he didn't want to follow these thoughts, Reece murmured, "In New York, it's well past your bedtime."

"Even in Surrey," she whispered. "Reece, how can I thank you? Do you see what you've done? You've healed me. Made me whole again. I want you so much, my body adores you, I feel so free with you…so wanton."

Emotion slammed through his chest like an ambush; she'd always had this knack of slicing through his defenses as though they were nothing but thin air. "The pleasure's all mine," he said gruffly; and knew that at some deep level he was evading her. "Maybe we should try and get some sleep—you've got a tree to decorate tomorrow."

"So I have," she said contentedly. "Are we having turkey on Christmas Day?"

"It's thawing in the refrigerator and Hazel's left at least ten pages of instructions."

"I cook a mean turkey," Lauren murmured. "Good night, Reece."

Her gaze was clear and guileless. She'd said nothing about love, he thought. He'd freed her body. But her soul was still in her own keeping. And wasn't that the way he wanted it? "I'll blow out the candles," he said, and climbed out of bed. One by one the soft points of light vanished, leaving only the dull glow of coals in the grate. Then, in the velvet darkness of a country night, Reece climbed into bed beside Lauren, put his arms around her and fell asleep.

On Christmas morning, Lauren woke late. She lay still for a few moments, hearing the small sounds of Reece moving around downstairs. They'd made love in the middle of the night in total silence, each anticipating the other's needs in a way that might not have been possible a couple of days ago. He was a wonderful lover, she thought, generous, ardent and sensitive. And wasn't that enough? Of course it was.

There was no reason whatsoever for her to feel this tiny edge of anxiety, this ripple of uneasiness.

Yesterday, they'd decorated the tree with ornaments that had been in Reece's family since he was a child; they'd made mince pies and a delicious curry. At midnight, they'd walked to a carol service in the nearby Norman church whose walls were over a foot thick and whose air breathed of all the men and women who'd found solace within those walls.

Reece was climbing the stairs; the fourth step always creaked. Then he came in, wearing jeans and nothing else, carrying a tray. "Breakfast," he said, laughter lines crinkling around his eyes. "Not sure it'd pass Hazel's eagle eye."

Mugs of coffee topped with whipped cream, fresh strawberries and peaches, and croissants hot from the oven. "Hey," Lauren said, "a man who can cook. I'd better hold on to you."

The words replayed themselves in her head. Hoping Reece wouldn't read anything into them, she sat upright, adjusting the pillows. Hold on to him? Her return flight was booked for just after New Year, and beyond that she had no idea what would happen. Reece wasn't saying. And she wasn't asking.

"I took the croissants out of the freezer and put them in the oven," Reece said. "Not rocket science."

They ate a leisurely breakfast. Then Lauren dressed in a cream silk shirt and wool skirt, and they went downstairs to put the turkey in the oven. Afterward, Reece plugged in the lights on the tree in the living room, lit the fire and turned on some music. Passing her a flat, rectangular package, he said, "Merry Christmas, Lauren."

She'd put her own package on the antique milking bench that served as a coffee table. Fumbling with the ribbon and paper, she drew out a wooden-framed photograph of a rocky beach edged with graceful cedars. The woman standing above the tideline beside a tumble of bleached driftwood looked lost in contemplation.

"But that's me," Lauren said.

"I took it after I left you there when we were kayaking, remember?"

"It's a lovely photo...is the frame homemade?"

"I took woodwork way back in public school. That's a piece of oak from an old shipwreck off the coast of Maine. I thought you might like it."

"I love it," she said and kissed him. "Thank you for not buying me something terribly expensive, somehow that wouldn't have felt right." Then she added eagerly, "You must open mine, you'll see why."

Hers was in a box, carefully wedged with tissue. He drew it out, removing the paper, to reveal a small wooden sculpture, a curve of driftwood shaped like a wave of the sea, from which emerged the sleek bodies of three killer whales. Gazing at it for a long minute, he said huskily, "We were thinking alike."

"I wasn't going to give you a sculpture, it seemed like cheating. But somehow I knew this one belonged to you." She added impetuously, "You see, what happened at the yacht club is forgotten. Behind us. You've more than made amends."

For a moment the leaping whales blurred in his vision. The words forced from him, he muttered, "You've forgiven me."

"Of course I have."

"I only wish I could forgive myself as easily—for Clea, I mean."

"Oh, Reece..." Lauren put her arms around him in a whisper of silk, feeling the tension knotting his shoulder muscles. "I went to the library and read about it in the newspapers...it was such a terrible tragedy. But it wasn't your fault. It could just as easily have been you who died, or anyone else. There's no defense against that kind of random violence."

He let out his breath in a long sigh. "You're right, I know. Or at least, my head knows. But if only I hadn't left her alone on the sidewalk."

In a sudden flash of insight, Lauren said, "That's why you had to go to Ecuador, wasn't it? To be as close as you could to the men who'd been kidnapped because you felt responsible for them. You were trying to make reparation for Clea."

"I suppose you're right—I hadn't thought of it that way. I did feel responsible for them, yes."

She said unsteadily, "You're a good man, Reece." And for once saw that she'd rendered him speechless. If only she could heal him as simply as he had healed her. But his wounds were deeper, she thought with painful accuracy. Deeper and more lasting.

He said roughly, "I'll always cherish your present, Lauren, it's beautiful."

"We were on the same wavelength—or rather, the same beach," she teased, wanting only to erase the strain from his face.

He got to his feet. "How about some champagne, along with smoked trout?"

"Just as long as we go for a walk before dinner."

"I'll drag you up hill and down dale and across a couple of English stiles."

So there was to be no more talk of Clea. "I saw some gloriously mouldy Stilton in the door of the fridge," she added. "The kind with big globs of green all through it."

He laughed. "I'll eat some, too. That way we can still kiss each other."

They kissed each other a great many times over the next three days. Kissed, made love, laughed, washed dishes, walked and talked. Twice they wandered over to the Queen Anne house, where Lauren was transported by Reece's collection of art; and where she met the housekeeper, Hazel, whose initial scrutiny of her amused her and whose subsequent friendliness was, she realized, in some way earned.

Lauren didn't think she'd ever felt so carefree, so happy and cherished. She loved being with Reece. And he, unless she was badly mistaken, felt the same way about her. He even looked younger, lighthearted in a way that touched her.

Except every now and then, when she'd catch him simply staring at her, his face unreadable, his eyes shuttered in a way she remembered all too well and thoroughly disliked. The next time she saw him doing that, she must ask him what he was thinking about. Even though she was afraid she wouldn't like the reply.

It couldn't be anything serious, she thought in a rush of confidence. Nothing could disrupt the wondrous happiness that enveloped her, day and night.

Enveloped her like Reece's embrace.

CHAPTER FIFTEEN

THREE days after Christmas, a driving rain kept Reece and Lauren indoors in front of the fire. Lauren was reading a novel she'd chosen from the eclectic array on the bookshelves, while Reece was trying to catch up on the newspapers that had been accumulating since they'd arrived. Turning a page of the financial section, he said lazily, "Have you invested the money from the house in Maine, Lauren? There are some good tips here."

She hesitated briefly. Then she said in a level voice, "I sent the entire amount to an organization in Chicago that looks after street kids."

He lowered the paper, his face inimical. "You *what?*"

"You heard. I did a lot of research first, and picked a very reputable group."

"You just couldn't accept that money from me, could you?"

"I couldn't keep money that had been stolen—tainted with fraud. It was really nothing to do with you."

"You're splitting hairs."

"Reece, we're arguing again. Let's not, please—not over money."

"You're so—"

The telephone rang in the hallway. He surged to his feet, the newspaper sliding to the carpet. "I'll get it."

Heartsick, she watched him leave the room. They hadn't had a single disagreement since she'd arrived; in fact, they'd been so perfectly attuned to each other that she'd let down all her guards.

She couldn't have kept Wallace's money. She couldn't.

Reece came back in, his face still closed against her. "It's for you. Your agent."

"Beth? I didn't give her your number, how did she track me down?" Quickly Lauren went out into the hall. "Hello?"

"Hi, Lauren, thank goodness I've reached you. I got your number from your landlord after swearing on a stack of Bibles that you wouldn't mind. Listen, the curator of the new art museum—you know who I mean, the one and only Maxwell Galway—is very interested in your latest sculpture, the one you finished just before you left. Unfortunately, he's leaving for Japan the day after tomorrow. Can you fly home? Right away?"

Her brain whirling, Lauren stared at the delicate grain in the oak paneling. This was the breakthrough that could launch her career; it was a huge honor to have one of her works even considered by the museum, let alone purchased. But how could she leave here? Leave Reece?

"Lauren? Are you there?"

"Yes...you've taken me by surprise, that's all."

"This is a chance in a lifetime, I don't need to tell you that. I'm sure you can get a flight tonight. Or tomorrow morning."

A sale like this would be a huge feather in Beth's cap, too, of course. "Can I call you back? In half an hour?"

"You're not thinking of turning this down? Maxwell Galway could make or break your career."

Suddenly angry, Lauren said, "Beth, I'm staying here with a friend, so there's that to consider, and I have no idea about seat availability. I'll call you back."

"Fine," said Beth, not sounding as though it was fine at all. "You know my number."

Lauren plunked the receiver down and stood very still

in the pine-fragrant hallway. Beth was right. She, Lauren, couldn't afford to turn this down. She really had no choice; she had to go back to New York.

Maybe Reece would go with her.

She hurried back into the living room and quickly explained the gist of the conversation. "I have to go. Maxwell Galway is one of the biggest names in Manhattan, I'd be a fool to pass this up no matter how it turns out. But I don't—"

"So you want me to pull strings for your flight?"

Reece looked frankly hostile. Lauren said strongly, "The last thing I want to do is leave here. But I can't afford not to go, don't you see?"

"I see that your art comes first. That's what I see."

In a flare of temper, she said, "So you can leave me to go to Ecuador but I can't leave you to go to New York?"

"Ecuador was a one-off thing. But you'll always be an artist, Lauren. And I'll always be second to that, won't I?"

"Always?" she repeated uncertainly.

Ignoring her question, Reece said in a hard voice, "I don't like coming second."

"Why does it have to be a choice? I'm a woman and a sculptor, both at the same time. You can't have one without the other, they come as a package."

"I'll call up and get you a flight."

Jettisoning any thoughts she might have had about inviting him to come with her, Lauren said, "So men can have a relationship and a career but women can't? I thought you and I were past that stage."

"I don't like being dropped the minute someone in the art world beckons."

"But this is important!"

"And I'm not."

"You're twisting everything I say. I really hate this," she said wildly and watched him stride out of the room.

From the hall she could pick up snatches of conversation interspersed with long pauses; ten minutes later, Reece walked back in the living room. "The only seat I could get you is tomorrow morning at eight-thirty. We're booked into a hotel near the airport for the night, so we'd better leave within the hour."

She looked around at the peaceful, firelit room where she'd spent so many happy hours. "I don't want to leave."

Reece said flatly, "I want you here for the next five days—not in Manhattan."

"Then come with me," she begged.

"I've got some clout—but I can't manufacture extra seats on a jet. Unfortunately, both my company planes are out of the country so that employees of mine could go home for Christmas. Besides, if I go anywhere, I should go to Cairo."

Her disappointment was so bitter that she felt a stab of terror. The one word that hadn't been mentioned in the last few days was love. Reece didn't love her and was completely averse to falling in love; so she'd better not get too dependent on him. Yet at some level wasn't she craving him to tell her he loved her? She heard herself whisper, "I'll miss you."

"We can keep in touch by phone. And we've got tonight. We should leave, Lauren, it's pouring rain and it'll be a slow drive into the city."

She said defiantly, "I want a kiss first."

"Do you?" he said softly, padding over to her.

His kiss was voracious, a blend of fury and desire that left her weak-kneed and trembling. Determined to hide this, she said lightly, "I'll go and pack. Or else we'll be making love on the carpet."

It took her less than ten minutes to throw everything into her suitcase; she wrapped Reece's gift separately, to carry onto the plane. Then she gave one last glance around the bedroom in which she'd found such felicity. Would she ever be back? Or was this the end?

Feeling as though her heart was being torn in two, she walked downstairs and found her cape and boots in the hall cupboard. Reece was talking to Hazel on the phone, explaining the change of plan. Then he ran upstairs, coming down a few minutes later in a business suit, carrying a leather overnight bag. He looked like a stranger, Lauren thought, a formidable stranger; and for the first time in her life wished she earned her living in some more ordinary way.

He took a black umbrella from the stand by the door. "Ready? We'll have to run for it."

"Reece—"

Something in her voice made him stop in his tracks. He said roughly, "Don't look like that, Lauren—"

"We'll see each other again, won't we?"

"Of course. We're not through with each other yet, you know that as well as I do."

It wasn't the answer she'd hoped for; but it was all she was going to get. "Let's go," she said with assumed calm, and reached for the door handle.

Although Reece was an excellent driver, the heavy rain took his total attention. Lauren sat quietly all the way to the hotel, trying to sort out the jumble of emotions that seethed in her chest. *Always,* Reece had said. And then, later, *We're not through with each other yet.* Yet. A small word with ugly implications. What exactly had he meant? Was she to become a long-term part of his future? Or was she to be discarded when he grew tired of her?

Had these few days of happiness been simply an interlude for him, rather than a building block to something more lasting?

There was another question, one her brain shied away from and to which she had no reply. Was she in love with him? Perhaps, she thought, gazing down at her linked hands in her lap, she was afraid of the answer.

The hotel enveloped her in the kind of luxury she'd read about but never experienced. Reece disappeared into the bathroom to have a shower before dinner; he didn't invite her to join him. She hung up her cream silk shirt, then discovered she must have left her toothbrush at the lodge. Grabbing her raincoat and purse, she wrote a quick note for Reece and took the elevator downstairs; she'd noticed a drugstore just down the road.

Somehow Lauren was glad to get outdoors and be alone, even if only for a few minutes. She hurried along the sidewalk, putting up Reece's umbrella, the raindrops rattling against the fabric like fire from a machine gun. The drugstore was almost empty. She chose a toothbrush, paid for it and pushed open the glass door. Absorbed in her own thoughts, she didn't even notice the young man who followed her into the rainswept darkness.

She and Reece would make love tonight, she thought, smiling to herself; they'd heal this rift that had opened so suddenly and unexpectedly. She couldn't bear to leave tomorrow with even a shadow of dissension between them. And she was being silly to doubt that she had a future with him; surely his sensitivity and care of her the last few days made that a certainty.

Out of the darkness a numbing blow struck her right arm. Lauren gave a startled cry, her purse dropping from her fingers to the ground. As she staggered, another blow grazed her cheek, landing on her shoulder, so that she was thrust against the wall that edged the pavement. The ribs of the umbrella scraped along the brick. For the moment there was absolutely no pain; as though it were all happening to someone else, she watched a thin young man with his hood pulled over his face grab her purse, run across the road, and vanish into the curtain of rain.

Her knees didn't want to hold her up. She found herself crumpled on the sidewalk, the skirt of her raincoat soaking up a puddle. Then, slowly at first, pain blossomed in her forearm and spread into her shoulder, throbbing with an insistence that made her grit her teeth. She lifted her other hand to her cheek, and saw with horror that there was blood on her fingers.

"Miss? What happened? You okay?"

The next few minutes were always confused in her mind when she looked back. Her rescuer, a brawny man in an old leather jacket, sheltered her from the rain and took a quick look at her cheek. "Nothin' to worry about," he said in rough comfort. "My buddy'll stay with you while I go call the police, won't take a minute."

Her weak, "Oh, please, no police," was lost in the beat of rain. His buddy, as skinny as he was brawny, said, "Lost yer purse, eh? Happens all the time, just be glad he didn't have a gun."

A gun. Clea. With sick horror, Lauren tried to gather her wits. She couldn't go back to Reece with blood all over her face, she must wipe it off. As she tried to reach in her pocket for a tissue, the pain in her arm made her whimper, and her hand wouldn't obey her. The skinny man said, "Here's the police. Don't you fuss now, they'll look after you."

In a blur of flashing lights, a police car drew up to the curb. A uniformed officer knelt beside her, rapping out a series of questions she did her best to answer; after which he helped her to her feet. And then a man in a raincoat, a man she recognized all too well, thrust himself through the small crowd of onlookers. "*Lauren*—what in God's name happened? Are you all right?"

"Do you know the young woman, sir?" the policeman asked.

"Lauren, answer me!"

She said weakly, "I'm fine. I was m-mugged, that's all."

Reece said rapidly to the policeman, "I'll get a doctor to take a look at her at the hotel. Do you have all the information you need?"

"Give me the name of your hotel, please, sir. Although I have to tell you there's not much chance we'll get our hands on the thief."

Reece rattled off his own name and the hotel's; then he put his arm around Lauren. "Let's go."

She said to her two rescuers, "Thanks so much for your help, it was very kind of you… Reece, you'll have to go on my other side, this one's sore."

As he took her left arm, she leaned on him heavily and walked the short distance back to the hotel. Their passage across the lobby was highly embarrassing: she did her best to ignore the discreet stares and whispered comments. Finally they reached Reece's suite. He closed the door and went straight to the phone. She said forcefully, "I don't need a doctor. I need to wash my face and lie down with two ice packs."

"You're going to see a doctor."

She bit back her retort and slid out of her wet raincoat. As Reece put down the receiver, she said, "The toothbrush is in my pocket, can you take it out?"

He bent to pick up her coat, taking out the small plastic bag. "The hotel would have given you ten toothbrushes—didn't that occur to you?"

So this was all her fault? "I didn't think of asking them."

"You didn't think at all."

"If we're going to have a fight, I have to sit down," she said, and lowered herself gingerly onto the king-size bed. "I'm truly sorry you had to see me with blood all over my—"

"How do you think I felt when I came out of the bathroom and saw your note, and then you didn't come back?" he said in a voice like ice. "The five minutes I waited felt like forever. And then when I went outside and saw the lights on the police car, I thought it was game over."

Her shoulder felt as though it was on fire and all she wanted to do was lie down and close her eyes; but she was too proud to plead weakness. "Well, it wasn't."

"No thanks to you. Why in hell didn't you wait for me if you had to go tearing around the streets at night?"

Lauren said overloudly, "I know this must be reminding you of Clea and that's why you're so angry. But give me a break, Reece—I didn't do it on purpose. I have no idea what the odds are of being mugged on a London street, but it was just plain bad luck, okay?"

"Yeah," Reece said in a staccato voice, "it reminds me of Clea. It reminds me of everything I learned that day on that sidewalk in Chicago. Not to let anyone else close to me ever again. Because it hurts too much when things go wrong. I was in danger of forgetting that. But not anymore. It's just as well you're going back to New York tomorrow—past time."

If her shoulder was on fire, her heart now felt as if it were encased in ice. "You don't mean that."

"I damn well do."

Her pride in shreds around her feet, she faltered, "You mean we won't see each other again?"

"There's no point. I shouldn't have forgotten the lessons I learned that day—and for that I'm sorry. This has been wonderful while it lasted, Lauren. But it's over now. Before either of us gets hurt."

A tap came at the door. Reece strode across the carpet, ushering in a gray-haired man in a wet raincoat who said briskly, "Dr. Huskins. A mugging? Atrocious that the streets are so unsafe—where did he hit you, madam?"

She'd never been called madam by a doctor before. As he examined her shoulder and washed her cheek, Lauren realized with an ugly shock that she hated Reece seeing her in her bra, her upper body bare. Hated being exposed to him and consequently vulnerable. Only this morning such a consideration would have been unthinkable.

The doctor recommended bed rest, ice packs and pain-killers, all of which she could have thought of herself. She thanked him politely, and as soon as he was gone, said, "I'm going to take a shower and go to bed."

"I'll order room service for you."

"I'm not hungry. I'll get a cab to the airport tomorrow, would you arrange that?"

"I'll take you to the airport," Reece said through gritted teeth.

"I don't want you to! You've made it horribly clear you can't wait to see the last of me. So order me a cab."

"I don't take orders and I'll drive you in the morning."

"Everything's got to be your way, hasn't it?" Lauren flared. "You can go to Ecuador and Cairo, you can tell me what to do with my own money, you can get rid of me when and how you please. Fine. Do what you like. But don't expect to ever hear from me again."

By a superhuman effort she managed not to wince as she got to her feet, and to walk to the bathroom in a straight line. For the first time in many days, she locked the door. Then she stripped off her clothes and looked at herself in the mirror. Dried blood had crusted under her chin, while her cheeks were as white as the sheets on the bed.

The last bed that she and Reece would ever share.

Her shoulder was a dull red; it was her eyes that looked bruised, she thought clinically. And why not? The world she'd shared with Reece all Christmas, a world she would have said was both drenched in ecstasy and utterly dependable, had fallen apart. In her heart of hearts, hadn't she believed that the intimacy between her and Reece could only grow deeper and stronger, binding them closer and closer as the days—and nights—went by?

But she'd been wrong. He'd opposed her flying to New York for the most important commission in her life, and then an act of violence in the rain had done the rest.

I'll cry tomorrow evening, she thought. Not tonight. Not tomorrow morning at the airport. And not in front of Maxwell Galway or Beth.

Or maybe I won't cry at all. Maybe instead I'll give thanks for a narrow escape from a man who's locked in the past.

Her mouth twisted. Who was she kidding? She'd cry her eyes out once she had time and privacy. But no one else had to know that. Least of all Reece.

CHAPTER SIXTEEN

IT WAS five o'clock in the morning. With a groan of dismay, Lauren punched down her pillow and pulled up the covers. She had a headache because for the seventh night in a row she'd cried herself to sleep; she was also suffering from heartache. She felt wretched. Rotten. Lousy. And, she thought miserably, sexually deprived into the bargain.

Not to mention lonely.

How could she, in so short a time, have grown so accustomed to Reece's body beside her, to the rhythm of his breathing in the dark? To his laughter, his incisive intelligence, his rapier wit? Not that he'd been laughing the morning he'd put her on the plane to New York. Far from it. He'd looked as though he couldn't wait to be rid of her.

She hadn't heard from him in the last week. Surprise, surprise, she thought ironically, burrowing her head into the pillow. For him it was over, and she'd be willing to bet he wasn't lying awake thinking about her. He'd probably already moved on to someone else. As an antidote to too much emotion.

The only comfort she could take was that she couldn't have done anything differently. She'd been herself with Reece. And he hadn't wanted her.

Her thoughts went 'round and 'round, in a way she deplored but was unable to halt. Finally, at half past five she got up, put on a pot of coffee and got dressed in tights and a sweater. As she poked around the scraps of metal and wooden blocks in one corner of her studio, desperate for an outlet for her emotions, she suddenly remembered the clay she'd bought the week before Christmas. Shaping clay had always given her pleasure. She grabbed an old cotton smock, pulled it over her head, and sat down at her table, a mug of coffee nearby.

Three hours later, Lauren pushed back her chair. The bust on the table in front of her had more or less made itself: she'd scarcely had anything to do with it. It was a portrait of Reece, infused with all his energy and decisiveness, faithful to the jut of his cheekbones and the strong line of his jaw. His eyes seemed to look right through her, discerning her most intimate concerns. I'm in love with you, she thought, and in utter astonishment repeated the words in her head. I'm in love with Reece Callahan.

Of course she was. Why else had she cried herself silly the very day she'd found out that Maxwell Galway was going to purchase one of her works? Six months ago she'd have been delirious with joy. But not now. Not when she couldn't share the news with Reece. Not when she was totally estranged from him, missing him achingly and unremittingly, in bed and out.

He didn't love her. He wouldn't allow himself to. But, frowning, she found herself wondering for the first time if he'd been afraid he might fall in love with her. Why else had he picked that ridiculous fight about her flying to New York, if at some level their intimacy hadn't scared him to death? And why else, in the cold flash of lights from the police car, had he looked at her with hatred in his eyes? His hands, she remembered suddenly, had been unsteady; he'd jammed them in his pockets when he'd caught her noticing them.

Could it be true? Had Reece sent her away so he wouldn't fall in love with her? Or was she building castles in the air because she couldn't bear the hard truth?

Her heart was fluttering in her breast like that of a trapped bird, and she found it hard to breathe. There was one way to find out. Ask him. Or tell him she'd fallen in love with him, and see what he said.

Lauren began pacing up and down her studio, her brain racing and her emotions in a tumult. She was being a total idiot to even think this way; wasn't it enough to have been so thoroughly rejected once without courting a second rejection?

Impulsively she picked up the phone and called Sam at his office in Boston. "Sam," she said without preamble, "do you think there's any chance Reece could be falling in love with me?"

"Happy New Year to you, too," Sam said. "Yes, I do."

"You *do?*"

"He certainly isn't indifferent to you. I was talking to him a couple of days ago and asked how you were—you'd think I'd asked about the wicked witch of the west... what's up?"

Briefly she described the events of the last week. "Where is he now, do you know?"

"In England. Staying in Surrey until he goes to Hong Kong later in the week. Why don't you phone him and find out if he's in love with you?"

"I have to see his face when I ask," she said edgily.

"I was supposed to fly to London around noon today. But the meeting was postponed and I haven't gotten around to canceling my ticket. You can have my seat."

"Oh, God," said Lauren, "I'm out of my mind to even think of seeing him again."

"We only go this way once."

Clea. Again. "All right," Lauren said, "I will."

"I'll square it with the airlines, luckily I do have some influence there—not as much as Reece, but enough. You'll pick up the ticket at the counter, okay?'' Quickly he gave her the details. ''Do you want me to phone him? Let him know you're coming? I could try and talk some sense into him.''

''No! No, I have to take him by surprise—that way maybe I'll find out what's really going on...wish me luck, Sam.''

''Right on. Let me know what happens, either way. Or if there's anything else I can do to help.''

''You've already done a lot, thanks so much. 'Bye for now.''

Lauren put down the phone. Absently she ran her finger down the throat of the clay sculpture to the curve of collarbone. What use was clay? It was the real man she wanted. The real man she was going to fight for. And hadn't she, unconsciously, infused his features with all the intensity he'd shown in their lovemaking? All the tenderness that she'd put her trust in? A film of tears distorting her vision, she realized she'd modeled the face of a man in love.

She'd take it with her; maybe it would speak to Reece in a way that she couldn't.

But if it didn't, at least she'd know she'd tried.

Many long hours later, Lauren stepped out of a taxi at the gateway to Reece's property. It was well past sunset, the trees barely discernible against the blackness of sky. ''Sure you want to get out here, miss?'' the cabbie said doubtfully.

She wasn't quite as sure as she had been. ''Yes,'' she said, smiling at him as she hefted the box with the sculpture under one arm and picked up her overnight bag. ''I'll be fine.''

He tipped his cap and drove off. Lauren walked through

the gate and along the driveway to the lodge, her eyes slowly becoming accustomed to the darkness. In the grove of oaks, a branch rubbed against another, squealing like an animal in pain; an owl hooted in the distance. Then she saw the lights of the lodge gleam through the trees.

So Reece was here. Although her relief, she noticed, was almost instantly eclipsed by an equally strong sense of dread. She had no idea what she was going to say to him. Or would she simply thrust the box at him and see what happened?

Steadfastly she walked on, the lights growing brighter. Not stopping to think, because if she did there was a fair likelihood she'd turn tail and run, Lauren marched up the steps and pushed the doorbell. Distantly, over the pounding of her heart, she heard it chime inside, followed by the sound of footsteps.

The door swung open. "Why, Miss Courtney," Hazel said, "what a nice surprise."

Swallowing a crushing disappointment, Lauren said, "Reece—he's here, isn't he?"

"Come in, come in, it's turned chilly, hasn't it?" Hazel said, and took Lauren's bag from her unresisting fingers. "Did you walk all by yourself up the lane? Now I've lived here all my life and that's more than I'd do. Mr. Reece? No, he left for London early yesterday morning. To fly to the States, he said."

"Yesterday?" Lauren repeated numbly.

"I believe so. Some emergency or other, he didn't say what. Or when he'd be home…are you all right, dear?"

Lauren put the box down on the nearest chair. So Reece had been on her side of the Atlantic yesterday and hadn't got in touch with her.

She had her answer. The one she'd come all this way

to find. As the heat of the hallway enveloped her, she said vaguely, "I'm fine, thank you."

Hazel pulled out another chair and eased Lauren into it. "You don't look well, if I may say so," she said. "You'll stay overnight, and I'll call Mr. Reece's office and find out—"

Roused from her lethargy, Lauren spluttered, "No, you mustn't do that."

Hazel's shrewd gray eyes sharpened. "Very well. But I'm going to get you a nice bite to eat and make sure you're settled in before I go back to the big house. Tom, my husband, will come by in the morning. You'll be comfortable here, by yourself?"

"Oh, yes." Lauren was craving privacy; and despite Hazel's genuine kindness was relieved when a couple of hours later she had the house to herself. Hazel had put her in the guest room; she didn't think she could have borne sleeping in the bed she and Reece had shared.

Restlessly she prowled through the house, picking things up, putting them down, feeling Reece's presence in every corner. She'd leave first thing in the morning. Go back to London and get the first flight home and do her best to forget a man who'd turned her life upside down, teaching her the joy and utter misery that was called love.

She found herself taking the clay bust out of its box and staring at it as though it could give her some answers. Carrying it downstairs and putting it on the coffee table, she sat down on the sofa. She'd deluded herself when she'd modeled the face of a man in love. Reece wasn't in love with her. He never had been.

Dazed with unhappiness, she burrowed her face in the soft velvet cushions. Half asleep, half awake, quite unable to gather the energy to go back upstairs, Lauren heard the antique clock chime each passing hour: ten, eleven, twelve, one. Then suddenly she jerked upright on the sofa, her heart leaping in her breast. Someone was turning a key in the lock.

The front door opened with the faintest squeal of hinges, slammed shut, and then footsteps marched along the hall. "Lauren?" Reece called. "Where are you?"

How did he know she was here? She faltered, "In the living room," and, as though it were all happening to another woman, watched his big body fill the doorway, his blazingly blue eyes trained on her face. She grabbed the bust, trying to thrust it between the table and the sofa, and said rapidly, "I shouldn't have come, I'm sorry, I'll never do this again and I'm going to leave first thing in the morning—"

"What's that you're trying to hide?"

His appearance in the middle of the night, so unexpected, so disconcerting, seemed to have loosed all the holds on her tongue. "I made it. I came here yesterday to tell you I love you, but I shouldn't have, you were in the States the day before and you didn't even call me, so I've made a complete fool of myself." Resorting to anger for a situation she had no idea how to cope with, she finished, "Why don't you just go to bed and forget I'm here? You're good at forgetting me, and I'll be gone by the time you wake up. Gone for good, this time."

He walked over to her. He was wearing a charcoal-gray suit with a blue shirt and silk tie; he looked exhausted. "Don't come near me!" she exclaimed, and clutched the bust all the tighter.

For a moment Reece froze in his tracks. "But you said you love me."

She thrust the clay bust at him. "When I made this, that's what I found out. But I have this stupid habit of acting before I think. Really stupid, under the circumstances, and not a mistake I'll make again.''

He took the clay piece from her, setting it down on the table and gazing at it. "When did you see my face like that?"

"Whenever we made love," she said defiantly.

"You saw what I've been blind to."

"I don't know what you mean…"

"I went to Cairo right after you left. Thought about you the whole time I was there. Came back. Couldn't stand being here on my own. Went to London—when the devil was it, the day before yesterday? I'm so jet-lagged I don't even know what day of the week it is."

He ran his fingers through his hair, his eyes glued to her face. "I stayed in the same hotel where you and I stayed, thought about you every minute of the day and night. So yesterday morning I got on a jet to New York. You weren't at your studio, your landlord didn't know where you were, nor did your neighbors. So I phoned Sam, who told me you were here, and told me—fairly forcefully—to smarten up."

Lauren said faintly, "Hazel told me you'd flown to the States the day before yesterday—that's why I was so upset."

"I was half crazy when I left here—didn't know what I was going to do." He glanced at the bust on the table. "The truth's been staring me in the face. But did I see it? No, sir. I was too busy protecting myself from feeling what the whole world feels—joy and pain. The happiness and vulnerability that comes from loving someone." He hesitated. "Do you know what suddenly hit me in the hotel in the middle of the night?"

She shook her head, suspense clamping her by the throat. "What?" she said baldly.

"That Clea was the last woman in the world who would have wanted me to shut myself off from loving you. She was very much alive in her short life—and she would have liked you so much, Lauren, I know she would have."

"I'm crying again," Lauren muttered. "I've got to stop this."

"I've been a fool, that's what I'm saying. I acted like a prize idiot about that cheque and about Maxwell Galway, because I knew I was in deep with you and it was time I put on the brakes. The mugging gave me a perfect excuse. End it. Send you home and go back to my nice, safe life."

So she'd been right, Lauren thought dazedly; Reece had been afraid of falling in love with her. Trying to get her facts straight through a surge of hope that felt like sunlight after rain, she said, "So you arrived in New York about the time I was leaving?"

"Yeah...if we'd met at the airport, we could have saved ourselves a lot of time."

"Time, money and grief. When I heard your key in the lock, I thought I was going to get mugged for the second time."

Making no attempt to touch her, Reece said hoarsely, "Lauren, I love you. That's what I'm trying to say."

She bit her lip. "I'm not dreaming, am I? Please tell me I'm not going to wake up in my studio to an empty bed— and an empty heart."

"I'm only sorry it's taken me this long to come to my senses," Reece said violently. "That I caused you pain when you're the last person in the world I want to hurt."

"You really do love me?"

Something like a smile lifted the harsh lines on his face. "Lauren, I really do love you."

She got up and walked right into his arms. "Oh,

Reece,'' she quavered, ''I love you so much. It's been so awful without you—hold on to me and never let me go.''

''I never want to let you go,'' he said fiercely, pressing her so close to his body that she could hear the pounding of his heart. ''You're all I ever wanted and ever will...and you even came looking for me after all I'd done to you.''

''You're worth it,'' she said with a radiant smile. ''Anyway, you came looking for me, as well.''

''We'll invite Sam—and his new girlfriend, he told me all about her—to the wedding.''

''Wedding?'' Lauren said. ''Aren't you getting ahead of yourself?''

He grinned. ''If you want me to go down on my bended knee, I will. Marry me, Lauren? Please?''

''Yes. Oh, yes,'' she said with a ripple of joyous laughter. ''You don't have to get down on your knees. But you could take me to bed. If you want to, that is.''

''Want to?'' he said huskily. ''You don't ever have to doubt that.'' He bent his head to kiss her, a deep kiss of passionate commitment. ''I'm yours, body and soul... you've made me whole again.''

''I love you so much,'' Lauren said, her eyes clear as rainwater, her face alive with happiness.

''Let's go to bed,'' he said. Picking her up in his arms, he carried her up the stairs into his room, where, in the big canopied bed, he pledged his heart to her in a lovemaking that carried Lauren to a place she'd never been before. A place they'd reached by literally making love, she thought; a place beyond words.

As she snuggled into his chest, her pulses slowing, she gave him a bemused smile. ''Do you have to tear off to Tonga or Tasmania first thing tomorrow?''

''I do not. Do you have to be on the doorstep of a

museum?'' He stroked a strand of hair back from her face. "I didn't even ask you about Maxwell Galway."

"He bought one of my works and I don't have to be anywhere else but here."

"So Galway's smart enough to recognize real talent when he sees it—congratulations." Reece gave her a lingering kiss. "As neither of us has to go anywhere, we could spend the day in bed. Planning our wedding, among other things."

"What about Hazel and Tom? They're supposed to look in on me in the morning."

"Hazel likes you. She'll be a model of tact and leave us strictly alone," Reece said, kissing Lauren with lazy sensuality.

And indeed, when Hazel unlocked the front door the next morning and saw Reece's suitcase standing in the hall, she backed up immediately, a big smile on her face. Then she hurried home to tell Tom to stay away from the lodge all day.

Pick up a Harlequin Presents® novel and enter a world of spine-tingling passion and provocative, tantalizing romance!

Join us in December for two sexy Italian heroes from two of your favorite authors:

RAFAELLO'S MISTRESS
by Lynne Graham
#2217

THE ITALIAN'S RUNAWAY BRIDE
by Jacqueline Baird
#2219

HARLEQUIN Presents

The world's bestselling romance series.

Seduction and passion guaranteed.

Available wherever Harlequin books are sold.

Visit us at www.eHarlequin.com
HPITAL

Three of your favorite authors will move you to tears
and laughter in three wonderfully emotional stories,
bringing you...

Mistletoe Miracles

A brand-new anthology from

BETTY NEELS
CATHERINE GEORGE
MARION LENNOX

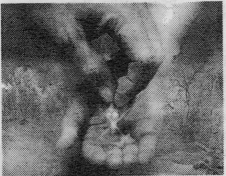

The warmth and magic of the holiday season comes alive
in this collection in which three couples learn that
Christmas is a time when miracles really *do* come true.

Available in November 2001 at your favorite retail outlet.

HARLEQUIN®
Makes any time special®

Visit us at www.eHarlequin.com

PHMBC

If you enjoyed what you just read,
then we've got an offer you can't resist!

**Take 2 bestselling
love stories FREE!**

Plus get a FREE surprise gift!

Clip this page and mail it to Harlequin Reader Service®

IN U.S.A.
3010 Walden Ave.
P.O. Box 1867
Buffalo, N.Y. 14240-1867

IN CANADA
P.O. Box 609
Fort Erie, Ontario
L2A 5X3

YES! Please send me 2 free Harlequin Presents® novels and my free surprise gift. After receiving them, if I don't wish to receive anymore, I can return the shipping statement marked cancel. If I don't cancel, I will receive 6 brand-new novels every month, before they're available in stores! In the U.S.A., bill me at the bargain price of $3.34 plus 25¢ shipping & handling per book and applicable sales tax, if any*. In Canada, bill me at the bargain price of $3.74 plus 25¢ shipping & handling per book and applicable taxes**. That's the complete price and a savings of at least 10% off the cover prices—what a great deal! I understand that accepting the 2 free books and gift places me under no obligation ever to buy any books. I can always return a shipment and cancel at any time. Even if I never buy another book from Harlequin, the 2 free books and gift are mine to keep forever.

106 HEN DFNV
306 HEN DC7T

Name	(PLEASE PRINT)	
Address		Apt.#
City	State/Prov.	Zip/Postal Code

* Terms and prices subject to change without notice. Sales tax applicable in N.Y.
** Canadian residents will be charged applicable provincial taxes and GST.
  All orders subject to approval. Offer limited to one per household and not valid to
  current Harlequin Presents® subscribers..
® are registered trademarks of Harlequin Enterprises Limited.

PRES01   ©2001 Harlequin Enterprises Limited

HARLEQUIN *Presents*

The world's bestselling romance series. Seduction and passion guaranteed!

Pick up a Harlequin Presents® novel and you will enter a world of spine-tingling passion and provocative, tantalizing romance!

Join us next month for an exciting selection of titles from all your favorite authors, each one part of a miniseries:

Red Hot Revenge
THE MARRIAGE DEMAND
by **Penny Jordan**
#2211

The Australians
FUGITIVE BRIDE
by **Miranda Lee**
#2212

Latin Lovers
A SPANISH AFFAIR
by **Helen Brooks**
#2213

9 to 5
THE BOSS'S VIRGIN
by **Charlotte Lamb**
#2214

Christmas
THE MISTRESS DEAL
by **Sandra Field**
#2215

Greek Tycoons
THE KYRIAKIS BABY
by **Sara Wood**
#2216

On sale November
Available wherever Harlequin books are sold.

Visit us at www.eHarlequin.com   HPGENNOV

Celebrate the season with

Midnight Clear

A holiday anthology featuring
a classic Christmas story from
New York Times bestselling author

Debbie Macomber

Plus a brand-new *Morgan's Mercenaries* story
from *USA Today* bestselling author

Lindsay McKenna

And a brand-new *Twins on the Doorstep* story
from national bestselling author

Stella Bagwell

Available at your favorite retail outlets in November 2001!

Where love comes alive™

Visit Silhouette at www.eHarlequin.com   PSMC

CALL THE ONES YOU LOVE OVER THE HOLIDAYS!

Save $25 off future book purchases when you buy any four Harlequin® or Silhouette® books in October, November and December 2001,

PLUS

receive a phone card good for 15 minutes of long-distance calls to anyone you want in North America!

WHAT AN INCREDIBLE DEAL!

Just fill out this form and attach 4 proofs of purchase (cash register receipts) from October, November and December 2001 books, and Harlequin Books will send you a coupon booklet worth a total savings of $25 off future purchases of Harlequin® and Silhouette® books, AND a 15-minute phone card to call the ones you love, anywhere in North America.

Please send this form, along with your cash register receipts as proofs of purchase, to:
In the USA: Harlequin Books, P.O. Box 9057, Buffalo, NY 14269-9057
In Canada: Harlequin Books, P.O. Box 622, Fort Erie, Ontario L2A 5X3
Cash register receipts must be dated no later than December 31, 2001.
Limit of 1 coupon booklet and phone card per household.
Please allow 4-6 weeks for delivery.

**I accept your offer! Enclosed are 4 proofs of purchase.
Please send me my coupon booklet
and a 15-minute phone card:**

Name: _____

Address: _____ City: _____

State/Prov.: _____ Zip/Postal Code: _____

Account Number (if available): _____

---

097 KJB DAGL
PHQ4013